Kafka in Brontëland and Other Stories

Also by Tamar Yellin

The Genizah at the House of Shepher

Tamar Yellin

KAFKA *in* BRONTËLAND

and other stories

The Toby Press

First Edition 2006
The Toby Press LLC

POB 8531, New Milford, CT 06776-8531, USA
& POB 2455, London W1A 5WY, England

www.tobypress.com

ISBN 1 59264 113 9, *paperback*

A CIP catalogue record for this title is
available from the British Library

Typeset in Garamond by Jerusalem Typesetting

Printed and bound in the United States
by Thomson-Shore Inc., Michigan

Contents

Return to Zion

M

y father, Odysseus, had a lust for travel, but after their marriage my mother Penelope insisted that he settle down. For many years he made three-piece suites in a furniture factory, but he never lost sight of his true desires. Each evening he spread the maps in contemplation of an epic voyage: across the Channel, through the French plains, over the mountains; down the Dalmatian coast, past the Greek battlefields to the port of Athens; by way of the Aegean to the Near East and the Promised Land. For my father, Odysseus—and many acknowledge this is a strange name for a Jew—dreamt all his life of the return to Zion, though what he would do when he got there remained a mystery.

Many times he assured me that I, his son, Telemachus, would not be left behind. No matter that by the time I was old enough to share his journeys we were exiled to the potting shed, where in cramped conditions and the smell of compost we trained our flashlights on the intended route. The floor was a mass of trampled charts, the walls a campaign; beneath the window with its dead geraniums lay the big atlas strewn with spider trails. Having traced the routes which seemed to us the most direct or most historical, we competed to devise the lengthiest and most fantastical: via China and the north pole, the West Indies and the Amazon; across the Himalayas and the top of Everest, through the dunes of the Kalahari with a retinue of geckos. We would travel by train, by caravan, by camel and by car; by ship, by barge, by liner and by junk. We plotted the course of the whitewater rafter and the hot-air balloonist, and touched down at a series of small airfields in our trip by Beechcraft across America.

Nor would the miles we covered be ignorant ones. We grew into students of survival, experts in terrain: we studied the etiquettes of clans and the customs of the natives. We would never leave ourselves at the mercy of ships and weather, unmade roads or erroneous maps; of the trickster guide or the wolf which lurks at the forest heart of Europe.

So we lost ourselves in the labyrinth of our preparations, an indefinite process in which the minutiae of timetables and forecasts, saints' days and seasonal winds were all-important, in which one must learn off by heart, night after night, the formal greetings of different peoples, the dietary precautions, the prevalence of snakes. It seemed that, if we ever did get going, we would require not only a pharmacy but a library on our backs; which was why my father insisted that we create a digest of all the knowledge we might need to complete our journey.

Was it possible to know everything in advance? The years were passing: timetables altered, ferries were cancelled, governments fell, even weather patterns changed. Islands were born and rivers died. Our great compendium was simply a hopeless task, a nitpicking procrastination.

Sometimes of a summer evening we would sit on the back step of the semi-detached, Ithaca, where we lived; my father would toss slug pellets on the garden and tell me stories of the ten lost tribes. Of Eldad the Danite from the land of Cush in eastern Africa, and Montezinus, who discovered the Hebrew-speaking Indians of North America; of the little red Jews beyond the river Sambatyon, and the black Jews of Abyssinia: all the lost Israelites who would return home only at the end of the world. Beneath a sky of brilliant stars I watched the slugs make their slow progress up the walls of our house and listened to my father's voice, that slow voice I now realise was laden with a great sadness.

When autumn came, we would pause by the big fire of leaves we had built in the garden and my father would talk about the Promised Land. About the rivers which flowed with milk and the rocks which cracked open full of honey. About the fig trees and oranges, the vineyards and olive groves, the former rain and the latter rain and the mass of flowers which spring up every year in the desert. About shining Jerusalem and the Temple covered with beaten gold.

"Solomon in his glory," my father said, crinkling his eyes; and we would adjourn to write up our log and ration out the strange, brain-shaped cheese my father called Macedonian Head.

Meanwhile my mother Penelope sat in the kitchen and discussed unguents with Mr Larry Cohen of the Aphrodite Pharmacy. His case of samples at his side, he applied various creams to her hands and massaged them in; from the kitchen window one might have supposed them to be plighting their troth, but the snatches of talk were quite innocent: "Now this is a light one, very light—" "It has a smell of magnolia—" "They really do use attar of roses—" My father entered, hands rank with poison and midges in his hair, and Mr Cohen, enquiring after his stiff back, would recommend the latest rubbing oils. Then he would leave, and in the void of his absence my mother would air her many grievances, for nothing reminded her of my father's shortcomings like the obsequious attendance of Mr Cohen.

Nothing, that is, except the benevolence of his brother, Mr Cyril Cohen of the Mercury Travel Agency, who regularly dropped by with brochures. His object was to tempt my mother to Bahaman islands and European cities, and I must confess, the bright pictures caught my fancy too. My father would return exhausted from the factory, and Mr Cohen would tell him of the latest offers on trips to the Holy Land. "No package tours," my father would say, wearily, and Mr Cohen: "But what you need, Mr Waxman, is a holiday. After all—" and here he winked at my mother—"Mrs Waxman needs one too."

My father would have none of it. The farthest he had travelled in my mother's company was to the beach, where he sat on the sand in his shoes and socks and read the newspaper. He would not take a cruise, or a coach trip, or fly by jumbo jet to a foreign capital.

"You'll see," he would say, "when the time comes," as we pored over our atlas in the stuffy shed, munching peanut brittle. He wrote up our logs and his writing resembled the journey of an absent-minded spider; nor did I ever suspect the grand futility of our plans. Meanwhile my mother ran here and there with her many suitors, but never attempted to break the ties which bound her to him.

Evening after evening we strained to pattern the definitive journey. We set deadlines and broke them, reset and broke them again: our calendar was a tangle of crossed days. We hibernated all winter in the creaking shed; we patched the roof with plastic when the rain came through. In summer the walls buckled and the door warped. We struggled on, our campaign collapsing around us.

Sometimes when my father leaned over to point I noticed how his hands were aging, the skin now knotted with sclerotic veins; and how his breath when he was hungry stank like an old man's breath. Time and again he lost his glasses beneath the heap of maps, time and again they were swept onto the floor. He mended the frames with tape, but he couldn't see: he accused whole towns of vanishing, he lost the route in a blur of other roads. As for me, I now felt the occasional twinge of a gigantic boredom. On occasion my father, with a melancholy glance, would leave the house by the kitchen door, and I would not follow; or when he came to fetch me in the early morning I would pretend to be asleep.

He was getting old; his hands were unsteady; he shuffled round the garden in slippers and a torn vest. At the furniture factory he cleared the bench and locker of thirty years and came home with a watch in his pocket, which for fear of noticing the time he never wore. He ate flapjacks in the kitchen and read newspapers; he talked of building a yacht, of learning to fly. *The Art of Boats* sat by his bed all summer, and the library books on navigation he was always forgetting to renew. He spent whole days in the greenhouse and the greenhouse burgeoned with thistles. Foxgloves filled the garden like a tall sea. Wood from the factory yard, and sheets of canvas, and nails and pots of tar were everywhere; hammers and saws, and his plane with the shiny handle.

It was a summer of storms, and often as I watched the rain I wondered whether, like Noah, he knew something we didn't. But later the sky would clear and fill again with stars. I stepped out into a night calmed and exhausted, warm and damp in the aftermath of storm, and standing on the back step I would watch the gleaming slugs, now dozens of them, now hundreds, climbing the crumbling walls of our house.

My mother sat in the kitchen with Dr Arnold Cohen, brother of the brothers Cohen: she had developed professional tastes. She told him about my father's blinding headaches and the blackouts. Dr Cohen examined my father through the kitchen window while she described the lapses of memory, the disorientation and the night-time fits. Dr Cohen said it was difficult to tell, but that my father was evidently suffering from something sinister in the head, yes, from a strangeness in the brain. The wind turned and the weather changed. The thistles burst and the thistledown flew.

It was the summer of my father's boat, the strange crippled boat without a prow which now took shape on our lawn. A boat in a sea of grass which would go nowhere. He asked me to help him, with a bad smile, knowing I was frightened, but without my assistance the boat grew higgledy piggledy, leaky and star-shaped, following a dozen different designs. He built a deck one day and dismantled it the next; started on the prow and was distracted by the stern. He sat on the back step with his tremendous headache and smoked cigarettes and contemplated the boat.

It was the summer of my father's boat, of the growing strangeness in his brain, of storms and heat and nights swarming with hot stars. I made drinks for the stream of suitors who sat at my mother's table and held her hand, and held her hand in the night while we waited for my father. We watched his light moving in the darkness of the garden: the glowing tip of his cigarette moving among the thistles. We heard the mechanical scrape of his saw, the beat of his hammer; neighbours knocked at the door and complained. When day came, he went to the local shops and lost his way. He threw bills and money in the dustbin.

In his pocket he carried the retirement watch which told him how late it was; one night he must have given in to temptation and looked. Out of the darkness we heard him cursing his own incompetence. He flung his hammer at the greenhouse. He attacked the potting shed with his mattock and saw. Early in the morning he made a huge bonfire of the potting shed and all its contents, on top of which he flung the skeleton of the boat.

Then at last the bed received him and my father slept.

For seven nights and days I sat at his bedside and listened to his slow breathing. I read him stories: about Rabbi Aaron Halevi, who travelled to the ten lost tribes through a sea of fire and smoke, and the Baal Shem Tov, tricked into taking a fast route to Jerusalem through quicksands. Softly, so no-one should hear, I sang him the song of the Babylonian exiles:

> *When the Lord brought us back to Zion*
> *We were like dreamers*
> *Then our mouths were filled with laughter*
> *Our tongues with joyous singing*
> *Then they said among the nations:*
> *The Lord has done great things for these people*
> *The Lord has done great things for us*
> *We were happy*

My father's bed was a boat on which he was sailing away, sailing away; I tried to explain why I had left him alone to take that journey. I wanted to tell him I would come with him now. But his eyes were closed, he heard nothing; he was sailing away, it was a calm voyage. He stood at the stern of the boat and he was not waving. He tossed his objects into the sea behind him: a lathe, an adze, a handsaw; a book, a cup, a pair of shoes.

> *Bring us back O Lord*
> *Like streams in the Negev*

Downstairs in the kitchen my mother sat with the three Cohens discussing the oddities of my father. All three Cohens shook their heads, bewildered.

"A pressure of blood on the brain," Dr Arnold theorised.

"Self-neglect," Mr Larry thought.

"But why not for God's sake take an aeroplane?" Cyril wondered.

My mother with the face of a grieving saint took my hand and whispered: "When this is all over, let's go away together."

Idly I browsed through the heap of coloured brochures with which she had been endeavouring to distract herself. America, Australia, Africa, Asia, Europe, the Far East—I tossed them aside one by one. I could summon enthusiasm for none of them, and I was suddenly panic-stricken at the thought of a world so shrunken there was no longer anywhere to escape to, anywhere to discover.

My mother Penelope drank wine with her suitors. This is a true story.

Kafka in Brontëland

M

y parents belonged to the lost generation, and when I was growing up their drawers were full of old letters, stopped watches, bits of broken history: a Hebrew prayer book, an unblessed mezuzah, nine views of Budapest between the wars. I drew pictures on the prayer book, mislaid the mezuzah, swapped the postcards for Peruvian stamps; and when my parents were dead and I was fully grown, I looked at the hoard and saw it was nothing but junk. Then I hired a skip and threw the lot—watches, pictures, letters and prayers—onto the heap of forgotten things, and came up here to start a new clean life; but I rattled the cans of the past behind me willy-nilly.

❧

There is a man in the village, they call him Mr Kafka. I do not know if that is his real name. He does not often speak to people. He is very old. Every day he walks down the village in the company of an elderly and asthmatic wire-haired terrier.

He does not speak to people. But he smiles occasionally: a faint and distant, somewhat dreamy smile. In this respect, but in no other, he resembles a little the Kafka of the photographs.

Derek the builder says that he is Dutch. Kafka is a Dutch name. No, no, I tell him, it is Czech, it is the Czech for jackdaw. It is like the writer Kafka, who was born in Prague. Who? The writer. Kafka the writer. The one who wrote *The Trial*.

Well, you never know, says Derek. And he tells me a story of how people die and come back to life. How young Philip Shackleton, who used to work at the quarry over Dimples Hill, fell into the crusher one day and disappeared. "Never found his body. Just traces of blood in the stones. Next year he turns up in Torremolinos."

The main question, however, is whether there are beams behind my cottage ceiling. Derek taps the plasterboard with his implement.

"Yes, I should think you've got a nice set of beams under there. Pine. Shall I go whoops with the crowbar?"

I say we had better wait a little.

When he has gone I dart across to the Fleece for a box of matches. Mr Kafka is sitting in the corner over a pint of dark beer. He wears a dirty mackintosh and a buff-coloured hat like James Joyce, and he stares into his beer as though time has ended for him. I consider making conversation, but I haven't the courage.

୨ଙ

When I was a girl I wanted to be Emily Brontë, but this summer I am reading Kafka with all the new enthusiasm of an adolescent. I walk the moors with a book, utterly entranced. I have fallen in love with him. Sometimes I imagine that I am him.

These literary obsessions are hardly innocent. My urge to be Emily, for instance, has altered my entire life. That is why I am here, alone in Brontëland. I grew up determined to live in passionate isolation. Only recently did I realise I had been misled: that she never spent a single day of her life alone in Haworth parsonage.

And now I have chosen to fall in love with Kafka. Kafka, child of the city. Kafka the outcast, Kafka the Jew. He wasn't inspired by spaces, he didn't belong in the hills. He didn't care for weather. He would have hated it here.

୨ଙ

Emily Brontë called these mountains heaven. Today they are referred to as the white highlands. Down in the valley, in the poor town, live the Asians, Pakistanis, Muslims from Karachi and Lahore.

Derek tells me about the first time he ever laid eyes on a black man. "I just stared." It was in the next village. "Not so exceptional now." "Yes," nods Hilda. "You don't see that many here still; but they're creeping up the valley road."

Hilda is a Baptist, Derek a Wesleyan; or it might be the other way round. They are always sparring. When she hears that I play the piano, she lends me a copy of *The Methodist Hymn Book*. "You're not the only Jew round here, you know. Mr Simons who runs the off-licence, I think he's half-Jewish."

I ask about Mr Kafka. Kafka, I say uncertainly, is a Jewish name.

"I thought he was Polish. Isn't he Polish, Derek?"

"Dutch," says Derek, with conviction. He lights his pipe. "Some sort of a writer fellow, so I've heard."

Then he tells a story about the Irish navvies who helped to build the reservoir. One of them, who was in love with the same lass as his neighbour, took the brake off one of the carts one day and ran him over, and they carried him up to the village, dead. "They said it was an accident," he concludes, "but you ask Ian Ogden and he'll always tell you, murder was committed in this village."

The Greenwoods and the Shackletons all have Irish blood. Derek's great-grandfather was a Sussex landlord. Hilda's used to make boots for Branwell Brontë.

※

Twice a week I ride down from the white highlands to the black town. In fact it is more of a grey colour. It has a shopping centre, a cenotaph and a community college. I am learning Urdu.

> *Ap ka nam kiya hai?*
> *Mera nam Judith hai.*

On Tuesdays I teach English to a young woman from Lahore. She is recently married: at the moment she seems to spend most of her time rearranging the furniture in the lounge. Every time I visit we sit somewhere else.

As a matter of fact her English is rather more advanced than my Urdu. She has a degree in Psychology. I decide we will read *Alice in Wonderland* together.

Mrs Rahim has lovely tendrils of hair at the nape of her neck, and I spend much of the lesson watching her play with them. I also stare at a framed picture of the Ka'ba done in hologram. The mad dream of Wonderland, taken at such protracted length, makes no sense whatever: we might as well be reading Japanese.

Mr Rahim pops his head around the door: a cheerful face, a white kurta. He is carrying a live chicken by the legs. Shortly afterwards I hear him killing it in the kitchen.

As I leave the house at five, the children are making their way to mosque to learn Koran: boys in white prayer caps, solemn little girls in long habits. I remember that a Jew should not live more than half a mile from a synagogue, to prevent the desecration of the Sabbath; nor can he pray the services alone. Ten men are required for a congregation; though they do say that a Jewish woman is a congregation in herself.

It is getting dark, and all the shops, the Sangha Spice Mart, Javed Brothers, the Alruddin Sweet Palace, are lit up like Christmas. I am filled with nostalgia for something I never had.

❧

Today I read the following lines in my *Introduction to Kafka*:

> More than any other writer, Kafka describes the predicament of the secular alienated Jew. Yet his work, so personal on one level, remains anonymously universal. He has no Jewish axe to grind. Nowhere in any of his fictions does Kafka mention the words Jewish, or Jew.

This seems to me remarkable. Can it be so? I resolve to make a thorough survey. There must be the odd Jew somewhere that my commentator has missed.

I cannot escape the impression that this is a pat on the back for Kafka. Yet they seem rather a sad conjuring trick, these disappearing Jews. A bit like that author who composed an entire novel without using the letter e.

The Brontë sisters did not recoil from mentioning Jews. I know all their references by heart. *Villette* has an 'old Jew broker' who 'glances up suspiciously from under his frost-white eyelashes' while he seals the heroine's letters in a bottle; but at least he does a satisfactory job. Charlotte describes her employers, 'proud as peacocks and wealthy as Jews,' but I have never liked Charlotte much. There is a 'self-righteous Pharisee' in *Wuthering Heights*, and in some ways I am grateful Emily did not live to finish that second novel.

The Brontës, of course, are often praised for the universality of their work. Especially *Wuthering Heights*, which is extremely popular in Japan. All of which goes to disprove our professor's thesis: in order to be universal you don't have to leave out the Jews.

※

I may change my mind about ripping down the ceiling in my cottage. It is a perfectly good ceiling, after all. A little low, perhaps—it gives the room a constricted feeling—but it covers a multitude of problems. Exposed plumbing, trailing cables, not to mention the dust, the spiders. And there may not even be any beams behind it.

"Can you assure me categorically that the beams are there?"

"Put it this way, I'm ninety-nine percent certain." Then Derek tells me how once, when he was pulling down a ceiling at Egton Bridge, he found a time capsule hidden in the joists. "One of those old tin money boxes with a lock. But it wasn't mine, so I gave it to the owner and he broke it open." What did they find? "A bit of a newspaper, five old pennies and a picture of a naked lady."

I say we will hold off on the ceiling for the time being. I ask him to tell me more about Mr Kafka. Has he lived in the village long?

"I can't rightly say. Have you seen his place? That cottage on back lane with the green door: looks like a milking shed. The one with thistles growing out of the doorstep."

In winter the thinnest trail of smoke came from the chimney. Sometimes the children played round there, but their parents didn't like it. Sometimes the old man tried to give them sweets.

No doubt the council were trying to get him rehoused. But, though he was a foreigner, he had Yorkshire tenacity: he wasn't moving for anyone.

I stop asking questions about Mr Kafka. I am suddenly embarrassed, as though by taking a special interest I have linked myself to him. It is a kinship I would prefer not to acknowledge.

❧

Not long before she got married, Mrs Rahim's father died. She nursed him herself for three months before the wedding. When he died she felt a great peace in her heart, as though she could sense him entering the gates of paradise.

Even so, he was always very close. Sometimes she was certain she could hear him talking in the next room. When she opened the door there was nobody there, but the room was filled with a feeling of warmth and love.

We are talking about death, and we are not making much progress with *Alice in Wonderland*. Death is less perplexing: we share many certainties regarding it.

"I think they are still here: I think they are listening," says Mrs Rahim. "My father suffered very much. But he is happy now."

Mrs Rahim reaches for her big torn handbag and brings out a man's wallet, worn, old-fashioned, foreign-looking. It is stuffed with papers covered in tiny handwriting. She clasps the wallet between her palms and holds it to her nose: sniffs deeply as though it is some redolent flower.

"I always keep it with me. It is like him."

I have a cold. She makes me milky tea boiled with cardamom, ginger and sugar. She slips a dozen bangles up my arm. Later, in an aura of almost sacred comradeship, we look at the Koran, which she carries to the table wrapped in a silver cloth.

She cannot touch it, she explains, because she is menstruating. Nevertheless I turn the pages for her reverently as she reads. She reads beautifully. I dare not tell her I am menstruating too.

ॐ

"Kafka. K-a-f-k-a. Kafka."
    "What sort of a name is that, then? Is it Russian?"
    "No, it's Czech."
    "Have you tried under foreign titles? I don't think we have any books in Czech."
    "He wrote in German, actually. But he's been translated."
    "Oh, look, it's here, Jean: someone must have put it back in the wrong place."
    A robust copy of *The Trial*, wrapped in institutional plastic: they leave me to it. Avidly I check the date stamps and the opening page.
    Why do I do this? It's a symptom of the literary obsessive: merely the desire to see the cherished works in as many editions as possible. As though one could open them up and discover new words, new revelations. I myself possess four different copies of *Wuthering Heights*. With Kafka, it is something else. I need to see which translation it is. This I can tell immediately, from the first sentence. "Someone must have traduced Josef K., for without having done anything wrong he was arrested one fine morning." I don't like 'traduced.' It's an immediate stumbling block. A lot of people don't know what it means. "Someone must have been telling lies about Josef K., for without having done anything wrong he was arrested one fine morning." That's better. Comprehensible. This copy is a traduced.
    I didn't expect the people of Brontëland would have much call for a book like *The Trial*. There would be a few lonely borrowings, half-hearted attempts, defeated best intentions. But I get a surprise. The label is a forest of date-stamps, repeated and regular, going back years: there are even a couple of old labels pasted beneath with their columns filled. I pick up *The Castle*. That will be different, I think: everybody reads *The Trial*. *The Castle* is, if anything, just as popular. There is a kind of frenzy in the frequent date-stamps which suggests, even, a profound need for Kafka in Brontëland.

It could all have been the same borrower, of course.

I leave the library with a strange reverence. It is as though the town and its cenotaph carry a peculiar secret, which I have stumbled on in the pages of a book. I see them for a moment with different eyes.

⁊ₑ

Having soaped my arm to remove Mrs Rahim's obstinate bangles, Hilda has lent me another book, *John Wesley in Yorkshire*. I thank her politely. I have not yet learnt any of the pieces in the *Methodist Hymn Book*.

My front door is open. Derek strides in, a big rangy man, and without a word he buries his pickaxe in my smooth white ceiling. It smashes up like papier mâché. He grins a long sideways grin.

"By heck, I hope I'm right about this."

He heaves at the plasterboard with all his strength and it comes crackling down, along with a shower of dirt and beetles which covers us both.

My beams are there. My revelation. The double crossbeam, backbone of the house: the ribwork of joists between. One has a blackened bite taken out of it where the oil lantern used to be. All are hung with a drapery of webs. Not so beautiful just now, perhaps: but when I have scrubbed them and scraped them, sanded and stained them, varnished them three times with tender loving care, they will be magnificent.

Derek stoops and picks out something from the heap of dirt: a piece of metal wrapped in a strip of cloth. "Old stays," he mutters. He raises his eyes to the ceiling. "Lady of the house must have been dressing herself up there," he says, "and dropped 'em through the floorboards. An heirloom for you."

He hands it ceremoniously to me. I use it as a bookmark.

⁊ₑ

When he has left I go for a walk on the moors. The sun is setting: lights are coming on in the valley. Someone is walking towards me down the moorland track.

20

It is Mr Kafka. He is following his slow dog down the hill to the village. He has nearly finished his walk, and his head is bent, contemplatively.

I wonder whether to acknowledge him. I am afraid to disturb his silence. He does not often speak to people. Sometimes he nods a greeting to those he knows.

As we pass each other my voice chokes in my throat, I can say nothing; but I manage a smile. Our eyes meet; he smiles back at me.

It seems a smile of recognition, and for the briefest moment he resembles once more the Kafka of the photographs.

The Other Mr Perella

T he first time he called up it was in the spring. My mother answered the telephone. She would not know him, he said, and he hoped she would not think him rude. But he had discovered our name while leafing through the local telephone book. He was investigating his family background, and wondered if there was any possibility of our being related.

We are rather proud of our name, which, while not unheard of in this country, is unusual enough to confer a little spurious mystique. In fact, his name was not identical to ours. It was spelt with only a single 'l', while ours had two; the pronunciation, however, was the same. Nevertheless, the lack of the second 'l' seemed to militate against there being any close connection.

My mother put on her best voice: Mr Perela had a deeply refined accent, and she was a snob. On the same grounds she was reluctant to reveal very much. Our own genealogy was hardly in Debrett, and she was not going to ask him if he was Jewish.

But that much was obvious. He plainly wasn't. And when, from her series of hints, he inferred our origin, his reaction was an explosive and delighted "Oh! But that is wonderful. Simply wonderful!" And he insisted that we come to visit when we were next his way.

"You see," he confided, in the course of their tumultuous conversation (we were soon to learn that waves of emotion crashed perpetually through the soul of the other Mr Perella)—"I know nothing about my own history, absolutely nothing."

When my mother put the phone down she was slightly breathless. My father, ever calm and analytical, commented: "He sounds a little mad."

"Yes," she agreed, her eyes moist, as though she really had just received a communication from a long-lost relative, from beyond the grave. "A little eccentric. A little desperate. But," she added, and this for her was the clincher, "he's a gentleman." It was largely at her insistence that we passed his way rather sooner than we might otherwise have done.

He lived in a large house near the sea, set back amongst tangled gardens on an isolated road. As we drove down the long rough driveway we exclaimed frequently, overwhelmed by the evidence of so much wealth.

So much former wealth, I should have said, for both house and grounds showed signs of having known better days. The windows were rotting in their frames, the garden a glorious wilderness; long strands of ivy trailed across the gravel and embraced the sundial near where we stopped. And the owner himself, who half ran towards us as the car drew up, was worn out like his property: bald and bespectacled, decent in a frayed waistcoat and faded corduroys, but curiously old-fashioned and neglected, like a man left behind by time.

He greeted us with the enthusiasm of a lost relation, pumped my father's hand, kissed my mother's, and professed himself charmed by the presence of three such beautiful children. I had never heard anyone speak in quite that way before. His Englishness was so exquisitely concentrated as to seem foreign.

The house smelt of mice and mould, and the narrow hall contained so many indeterminate objects we were obliged to squeeze our way through; in fact the entire place was crammed with junk and clutter like a vast attic. Our host flung back the door on room after room. We glimpsed tapestries, uniforms, weapons, a stuffed moose head, a hurdy-gurdy. Finally we reached a wide, sunny living room with French windows and enormous pictures; there, on a broken-down chesterfield strewn with Indian shawls, were two children, older than us: a boy and a girl, as untidy as everything else. The girl wore a buff-coloured smock and purple stockings, and had long unruly hair; the boy lounged against the back of the sofa with his hands thrust into his trouser pockets, gazing at us through a donkey-fringe. Mr Perela introduced them as Miles and Flavia, his children; and while Miles tossed back his hair and flung out a hand to be shaken, Flavia bounced out of the room to fetch tea.

An unaccountable silence followed. Mr Perela gazed uneasily at his son. Then he said, without preamble: "For God's sake, Miles, sit up straight. Don't they teach you deportment at that bloody school of yours?" The words were spoken in a bantering, half-humorous way, but we were none of us deceived. Miles looked sulky and shifted an inch in his place; my mother began very quickly to make small-talk.

Flavia had baked a ginger cake in honour of our coming. As she set out the tea things and handed round plates, I admired her completely adult poise. She must have been about fourteen, but she had the gestures of a woman, spoke like a hostess, and displayed not the least hint of diffidence. Even her untidy red hair seemed deliberate, fashionable.

After tea we left the adults to themselves and explored the house. Miles disappeared off almost straight away. "He and father hate each other," Flavia said. "It's a bore." We played the hurdy-gurdy; it produced a blurred, chaotic sound, at once comical and sinister. She began tossing things out of an old ship's chest: a wig, a doll with a soft body and china face, a pasha's switch made from a horse's tail. Everything here was touched by ghosts and belonged to the past. Flavia herself was ghostlike, other-worldly.

I picked up the switch. "Are all these things yours?"

"They're father's. He collects them. He goes to auction sales and buys mountains of other people's junk." She made a mock yawn. "He's such a bore about it!"

She took us up to her bedroom. It was cold, and to my notions, miserably bare. Flavia bounced onto the bed, and, to our well-concealed astonishment, pulled a squashed packet of cigarettes from under the pillow. "Do you smoke?" She shrugged her shoulders as she lit up. "At my school literally everyone smokes. You can't really avoid it." While I examined the items on her dressing-table—lipstick, powder, earrings, a string of hippy beads—she talked to my sisters, who made a pretence of being more worldly-wise than they were: how her parents were divorced, how she attended boarding school, how she spent the Easter holidays with her father and Christmas with her mother. As she leaned back against the wall I noticed the gleam of a gold cross against her throat.

We ran outside into the garden.

The idea was to find Miles and torment him, but there was no sign of him in the broken greenhouse, on the wrecked tennis court or in the woods. The floor of the woods was scattered with narcissi and nascent bluebells; they sloped a little in the direction of the cliff, and looking back at the house it too seemed to lean forward slightly, as though the whole property were sagging gently towards the sea.

I lost the others and found Flavia on the cliff. "Look," she said, pointing. "You can see the moon." Its pale three-quarters hung against the clear blue sky. "Do you think the moon is a man or a woman?" she asked.

"A man," I answered decidedly.

"Oh, no, she's a woman!" She frowned. "Sometimes I talk to the moon. Sometimes I talk to her all night. I pretend she's my mother." She turned to me with an appraising look. "Do you think we're related?" I shook my head. "No, I don't think so either."

When we returned to the house the grown-ups were already on the whiskey and sherry. My father, who never drank, looked awkward cradling a cut-glass tumbler in his hands. The other Mr Perella was leaning over my mother, who turned the rough-edged pages of an enormous book.

He looked up and his eyes crinkled behind his round glasses. "I see Flavia has been performing the role of hostess," he said, adding severely: "Splendid, splendid."

All the way back to the city we discussed the idiosyncrasies of the other Mr Perella. He was both quintessentially English and essentially foreign. He had attended minor public school; fought in Burma; endured a disastrous marriage. For years he had tried to trace his family without success. Now he was, as he put it, 'alone.' His children did not seem to figure in this isolation. Pouring out his heart to my mother, whom he found immediately sympathetic, he confessed that his life was ending as it had begun: in exile.

"As Jewish people, I am sure you understand," he had concluded. And then he added: "But you have so much history. I envy you your history."

This flattered her. She had already constructed many romantic notions around the English aesthete, the well-educated exile with the impeccable accent and the blank past, the lonely house on the clifftop crammed with mementoes of other people's lives. In the lights of the passing traffic my mother's face glowed and darkened with the mystery of it all.

੨੬

Some time later, the other Mr Perella came to visit us. He came alone. My mother dressed up the spare bedroom to receive him.

I believe there was some disagreement between my parents over the wisdom of taking this course. My father was not enthusiastic. He had few romantic illusions, and feared our guest might outstay his welcome.

The other Mr Perella looked taller and more fragile out of the context of his house, and more than ever like a visitant from another time. He gave off a peculiar odour too, not a human smell at all, but one of damp wood and dust: the smell of a genuine relic. Meeting me again, he graciously kissed my hand. I giggled; he did not smile. Rather he looked disgusted.

He stayed for a week. To a child—perhaps also to a host— this seemed an inordinate length of time, long enough to feel as if I should always come home from school to find him reading, his finger pressed to his brow, under the standard lamp in the corner of the lounge. I got used to his smell and his green waistcoat and the fragments of black hair—nose-clippings—which he left in the bathroom. He listened to me play the piano with a concentration I had never felt from my teacher, and made me recite, under the standard lamp, the things I had learned in school.

"So you want to be a writer," he reflected, passing his fingertip over the bridge of his nose. He never looked at me directly, giving off an air of diffidence, even fear, which I was too young to interpret. "In that case there is a book you must read. It is the greatest novel ever written, and no-one can be a good writer unless they have read it. I will lend you my copy, but only on the understanding that it is a loan and not a gift. It was given to me by a very dear friend who is dead, so you must absolutely promise to return it." He brought out the book, which was not so much thick as heavy with the weight of hundreds of tissue-thin pages, and had a green cover embossed with gold. He showed me the dedication, written in already faded ink: From Charles Douglas to Anthony Perela, June 1944. I accepted it with the understandable reluctance of a child accepting a book which they must both read and return. It was *The Charterhouse of Parma*.

What was his history, what was his secret? Perhaps he had none, and the days my mother spent chasing embassies and writing letters and investigating records, unknown to me, were wasted on a man who had no secret and no history, a man from nowhere. A man whose very identity was his need to belong.

❧

He did not visit our house again. Sometimes he telephoned. "Oh," my mother would say, her hand covering the mouthpiece, "it's the other Mr Perella!" Over the years we saw him occasionally, always, it seemed, on impulse or by accident, so that I never happened to have *The Charterhouse of Parma* with me and was unable to return it; but more than this, I was unable to do so because I had not read it yet. At every encounter I sat rigid under expectation of being asked about the book.

My mother grew older, was widowed; he grew older, grew ill; they shared not only a common affection but a common understanding of the cruelties of time. His children were adults now: Miles had gone off to India with a backpack and Flavia was something Bohemian in London. He continued to seek out putative relatives in Paris, Rome, Amsterdam; he created a network, a directory of Perellas, even discovered a branch of our own family we did not realise we possessed, but he never found any who would own him as kin. The last time we saw him was at the Royal Hotel in Scarborough, in their elegant dining room. It was the perfect setting; he and my mother talked until the remnants of the buffet were cleared away and the waiter swept the floor with an old-fashioned roller. He looked ill, obviously and slowly dying. Towards the end of their conversation he put his fist gently to his chest—he wore the same green waistcoat, I noticed—and said, in his husky, learned tones:

"I suppose what I find so hard to accept is that I am really going to die without ever knowing who I was. I mean, I should be old enough to accept that by now." And after a moment he repeated, with lowered eyes, "One should really be old enough to accept these things."

My mother must have grown to love him, this relative who was not related, this lost Perella. She placed her hand over his. It was one of the few occasions on which he permitted himself to be touched. "What nonsense, you know exactly who you are," she said, smiling. "Stop looking for evidence that you're someone else."

He gave her a sharp look, and after a moment he removed his hand.

There was a finality in that last good-bye. My mother was weeping a little. They knew they would not see each other again.

Dimly I sensed it too. "I never gave him that book back," I said as we emerged from the gilded splendour of the foyer into the chilly afternoon.

"I wouldn't worry about that," my mother replied.

And indeed I still have it, on permanent loan. It seems to me, on the rare occasions when I pick it off the shelf, that the burden of guilt makes it peculiarly heavy. Perhaps this was one of the few things he possessed which were actually his own; and he gave it over into the irresponsible hands of a child. There is no comfort in pretending that he would have wanted me to keep it, since he stated categorically that he did not. Nor can I help wondering about the consequences, for my writing skills, of the fact that it is still unread. But in this respect, perhaps, it only represents the withheld revelations of all the other unread books.

At least, whenever I look at it, I remember him.

The Girlfriend

One image will remain in my mind forever from that day. It was when my brother appeared at the door and the door opened, and he stood on the threshold, swaying slightly. His eyes were glazed, like a zombie's, and his lips were moving but no sound emerged.

I had never seen him drunk before.

Of course, at the time, I did not know he was drunk. I know now, looking back; but then I was too young to know anything much. Which is, perhaps, why the image remains so strong in my memory. So far as I could tell my beloved brother was desperately ill, damaged, destroyed—a zombie who did not recognise me any more. He pushed straight past me and stumbled into the house, as if I didn't exist.

Later, I found a puddle of vomit in the back garden.

"Your brother isn't feeling well," my grandmother explained, confirming my suspicions. "Don't bother with that, he had a little accident." And she hustled me into the kitchen, where a bowl of oily chicken soup was waiting.

My grandmother's kitchen was small, and haunted by the burnt dinners of the past. I felt safe there. It had a big old-fashioned fridge, painted units with red plastic handles, and a table covered by an ancient oilcloth. There was a walk-in pantry which smelt of—what? Preserves? Butter? Mothballs? A mixture of all three, perhaps, bound by the indefinable smell of my grandmother.

I sat at the small table which faced the wall, and obediently ate my soup. There was an old JNF calendar on the wall from 1972, kept I suppose because my grandmother liked the picture. Flowers of the Negev. Together we will make the desert bloom.

My grandmother pushed me on the shoulder.

"Eat bread with it," she said.

Below the calendar were the brass candlesticks she brought from the shtetl, standing on a steel tray; one of them was held together with a matchstick. I knew she never lit them. She couldn't even say the proper words.

The chicken soup was pale, clear and golden, full of tiny noodles; but it had no flavour.

The kitchen window looked onto the back garden. The sun was shining. Upstairs I could hear my brother walking about. Everything was just as usual, and there was a catastrophe hanging in the air.

❧

My brother was a good deal older than I. Ten years older, to be exact. I was the baby of the family, and consequently to be sheltered, petted, teased and spoiled.

I see pictures of myself sometimes, resplendent in frills, my head topped by an enormous bow. I sit like an expensive doll in the arms of my brother.

When I was five he built me an Airfix aeroplane and hung it over my bed. When the light went out it hung protectively above me, an image of him.

We played records on the old gramophone. I changed the records, he performed: in front of the full length mirror, with his flares and his long hair, he played air guitar with all the passion of his adolescent soul.

My father looked up from his paper and said, "Is that the baby, playing records?"

I watched with fascination the distended limbs, that painful distorted face. It was the first hint I received of the passion of which he was capable.

A pity my parents did not come and watch the show. It might have been a revelation to them. Meanwhile they expected an entirely different sort of performance from their son: prizewinnings, examination honours, an academic highwire act. And up to a point, he delivered.

There is another picture I still keep, of my brother in his bar mitzvah suit. I retain it mostly out of disbelief. In his yarmulke and tallit he looks like someone else's brother. I cannot comprehend how he held that pose, while they took the photograph, or how he still holds it so obediently. Later events should have erased the image.

It was shortly after this that he went into freefall. The term following the bar mitzvah all his marks were down. That summer his teacher called in my parents to tell them that he was disrupting class.

It came as a complete shock to them.

I know the whole story by heart now, from their lips. It has been repeated as a warning and example many times over the years. How lucky I have been, to have such experienced parents, to have had a brother who could be set up as a warning and example of the way I should not go.

※

My grandmother said, "Eat your ice cream, it'll get cold." She always said this. I always smiled.

We raised our eyes to the ceiling, where there were still traces of the Fray Bentos pie that had once exploded. My brother was no longer pacing around.

"Eat it," she reiterated, flicking me with the tea-towel.

My grandmother's house backed onto the park. If you squeezed through the gap in the hedge you were in the bluebell wood below the golf links. My grandmother, who was no longer capable of squeezing through anything, went round the corner to the proper entrance. She walked in the park every day of her life, with or without breadcrumbs. It was her park. In my ignorance I believed the park belonged to her.

Most Sundays we took a turn around the lake together. She greeted a number of other elderly people whom she knew by sight, or from the Reform synagogue where she went for free wine and cake after the sabbath service. In between whiles she quizzed me on what my mother was up to.

"Have you been out much this week?" I would give a dutiful child's account of my parents' comings and goings. "Had any visitors?" She glanced at my favourite dress, which my mother had given an extra lease of life by adding a hem of broderie anglais. "Did your mam do that?" My grandmother missed nothing.

She lived alone now, and seemed content. Her husband, who had coughed on his pipe in a corner of the sitting-room for six years and died, was only a vague fear in my memory.

When we got back to the car park she always bought me an ice cream. Sometimes she made cryptic remarks about my brother. "She should leave him alone. The silly woman." What did schoolwork matter? It was the rebels who usually made money in the end. Then she muttered, "Poor lad," and, pressing the pain in her side, like a low wheeze, "*Choleria.*"

ॐ

Escaping cholera and pogroms, she had come to England from Poland at the age of ten, to be obliged at twenty into a marriage she didn't really want. At the age of seventy she began lessons in reading and writing, by which time it was almost too late: her eyesight was bad, her hand so unsteady she could barely form the letters.

The girl who taught her was a nice girl, though. After the lesson they sometimes shared a glass of Irish cream liqueur.

It must have caused her some bewildered pleasure to have such an academic daughter. Proud she must have been: why else would she have kept my mother's school reports in a special envelope? Yet she was also a little wary, a little scornful of this illustrious stranger, her daughter.

The scholarship was one thing; that was all very well. Once you had your school certificate, though, and all those prizes, what could you really do? Take a course in shorthand typing and book-keeping, go down to London and find a secretarial job, get married. Which is what my mother did, of course.

Though she didn't have to go and marry that foreigner, my father.

Yes: my grandmother, the foreigner, resented the foreignness of my father. A Jew, maybe; but what sort of a Jew! From Africa or Argentina or somewhere, she couldn't remember what. She didn't know such Jews existed. A Litvak would have been almost better.

Also, a dreamer with a strange manner. He gave you the impression he was never quite here. Would he make money in the family? No. Too busy with his dreams, to go here, there. A Zionist, even. (A wave of the hand, a roll of the eyes.)

He himself had never acquired a proper education. But with all those genes the grandchildren were sure to turn out something special. And these days they could be properly educated, an English education, they could make something of themselves. Never mind their dreamer of a father, their over-ambitious mother. Such children would find their own way. But you mustn't push them. You must let them work it out for themselves. And don't keep on reminding them how they are Jewish.

※

The year my brother went into freefall, my parents began laying their plans to emigrate. I don't remember which came first. I was very young at the time.

My father looked into the possibility of selling the business. My mother conducted a lengthy correspondence with our friends in Israel. Figures were calculated, proposals drawn up. Someone even put in an offer for the house.

Of all the inconvenient times to go, this seemed to be the least inconvenient. I was still very young. My education could still be saved. (Though it wouldn't, of course, be an English education.) My brother was more problematic. He was about to begin his O-Level courses.

He would have to learn Hebrew almost from scratch: his bar mitzvah pieces he had only parroted. Why not begin lessons now?

I remember him attending evening classes, driven by my father across town to the Hebrew Circle. I remember the winter evenings, dark; the two of them in their overcoats, my brother carrying his school briefcase.

While they were gone I ate a chocolate truffle and watched *Kung Fu*. My mother said I would pick up the language in the first six months.

Three years later, when she dragged me bodily to the local Talmud Torah, I wept; but within six months I was racing my way through Exodus. My brother never got further than asking for a cup of coffee.

୬

My mother married my father against the wishes of her parents. And who can blame her? He was young, idealistic, good-looking. She was young, idealistic, good-looking. They went on political marches and looked good together. Later they supported each other in the renunciation of youthful ideals.

I do not say these things merely to criticise. I am just intrigued by the hypocrisy of the generations. As I grow older I watch for signs of it in myself.

Actually I regard my father as a tolerant person. People say he is a shy man, but what they call shyness I recognise as the circumspection of the foreigner. He has been foreign for most of his life. My mother has always stood as interpreter between him and England.

In many respects he has been the victim. He has been the victim of a terrible misunderstanding between himself and the world. The world expected him in one place; he turned up in another. In this, my mother was the unwitting facilitator.

All his life he has believed that by going to Israel the misunderstanding could be put right. The sad fact is that he would be a foreigner there too.

୬

Every Thursday evening my parents went to learn Hebrew at the Hebrew Circle. They left me at home in the charge of my brother.

(Now this is what I remember about my mother, preparing for the Hebrew Circle: how she carefully made up her face, and fastened her hair with a Spanish comb; how she put on the black coat with the fake fur collar, which usually she only wore to dinner parties. She was making herself up for the part, the part of the intending emigrant she was then playing. From childhood she had loved drama.)

At first my brother and I played Ludo and Monopoly and had cushion fights, and when the car headlights rounded the gate at ten o'clock, he packed me off to bed. Later he spent more and more time eating peanuts and talking on the phone.

Then one evening the doorbell rang. My brother escorted a tall, long-legged young woman into the lounge.

I was sitting on the floor in my pyjamas watching television. The young woman stood in the middle of the room clutching her handbag with both hands, like an awkward guest.

"Say hello, this is Trish," my brother said.

She smiled down at me.

"Hello," I said.

Trish threw my brother an imploring glance. He hovered uneasily between the door and the sofa.

"Sit down," he said, and left the room. She sat, like an interviewee. I stared at her.

"What's that you're watching?" she asked.

"*Tomorrow's World*," I said, without taking my eyes off her face.

She smiled awkwardly again. My brother reappeared with two cans of beer. He jerked his head.

"*Oi*. Bedtime."

But Trish interceded. "Oh, let her stay awhile. It's early yet."

I soon found myself sitting between them on the sofa, sipping beer from my brother's can.

"She likes it," he said. Trish giggled.

Trish had lovely soft gold hair, like doll's hair, and beautiful long red nails. She wore a soft blouse with the top three buttons undone, and a short wool skirt. There was a gold chain glinting against her throat.

"You smell like a hairdresser's," I said.

"Maybe that's because I am a hairdresser." She winked at my brother. "What lovely long hair you've got. Would you like me to do you a French plait?"

My brother put on some music and fetched more beers while she brushed out my hair. It felt strange and pleasurable, having this strange woman's fingers in my hair. Afterwards when she held the mirror behind me, just like a proper hairdresser, so I could see the plait, I was filled with a sudden surge of fear and desire.

Later they danced to the music and I watched, sleepy with beer, until my eyes closed. Someone lifted me up and carried me to bed. My last sensation was of somebody's fingers in my hair, hastily undoing the folds of my lovely plait.

⁊⋆

After that, Trish made regular Thursday visits. My brother told me I wasn't to breathe a word to our parents, and difficult as this proved to be, I tried my best.

Sometimes she brought me a small gift in her handbag: a comb, some beads, or a creme egg. She took me off into a corner and gave me them in secret, when my brother wasn't looking. For some reason the gifts displeased him.

Once she brought a bag of heated rollers. For over an hour she sat laboriously curling my long and voluminous hair. The warm teeth of the rollers dug into my scalp. When they had cooled, she let out the curls and I looked at myself in the mirror: a stranger with a head of glorious shining ringlets. Trish smiled at my shoulder.

Later, in the darkness of the bedroom, I heard them quarrel.

The next morning my mother said, "Goodness me, your hair is getting curly!"

I swear by my life, I didn't say a word.

I hid in the bedroom most of the day, to escape the shouting. Trish never turned up again after that, and Mrs Galinsky came to babysit.

⁂

The litany of warnings, repeated over the years, grew into a sort of folklore between my parents and myself. Gradually I came to recognise that nothing I could say or do, no prizes I could win, no qualifications I acquired, would free me from the ghost of my brother's failure.

One tale in particular my mother liked to tell. Like an early martyr pressing shards of glass into her palms, she told it again and again.

My brother stayed out night after night, drinking. Running around with his *goishke* friends, whatever he did. One night he told my parents, "I'm going out." My mother said, "If it's too much to ask where you're going, can we at least ask what time you'll be coming back?" He seemed to see reason for a moment then, almost to see his duties as a son. Because he said quite reasonably, "Look. I'll be back by midnight. I promise." And he went.

Midnight came, my parents waited up. No sign of my brother. One o'clock, my mother went to bed. I'll wait for him, my father said. Two o'clock, he comes into their bedroom, wakes her up. I'm really worried, he says. Maybe I should call the police? Give him a little longer, my mother says. Half past three, my father's sitting in the kitchen in his pyjamas, he's crazy with worry, he believes his son is dead in a ditch by now. The door opens and in walks my brother, drunk.

"My God, where have you been?" my father cries.

He shrugs his shoulders. "Out."

"But you promised," my father says, "to be back by midnight. Do you know how long I've been sitting here, worrying myself to death? Why do you do these things to me?"

My brother looks him straight in the eye and says, "Because I hate you."

And at this point my mother repeated the hackneyed phrase which was like digging shards of glass into her palms, which never lost the power to lacerate even after fifteen, twenty, thirty times: my father came into the bedroom and laid his head in her lap, and cried like a baby.

⊰⊱

Yes, she implied, my brother was very well educated in two things: how to hate his parents, and how to drink.

In six years at the Talmud Torah I learnt to know and love the Hebrew Bible, the prayers, the songs and the Jewish rituals. In six months at the Hebrew Circle my brother learnt to ask for a glass of beer.

"*Birra, bevakashah.*" He sometimes ordered beer in Hebrew as a joke, from the bartender at the Queen's Head, round the corner from my grandmother's.

Une bière à la pression, s'il vous plaît, una caña por favor, una birra, ein Bier, bitte.

He was not unintelligent. He knew how to order beers all over the world.

⊰⊱

I was just finishing my ice cream and my grandmother had put the kettle on. And a car pulled into the drive: we saw its shadow behind the frosted glass of the door.

"Hellfire, it's your mother," my grandmother said. "Go into the front room, quick."

"Why?"

She chivvied me out with damp hands. "Don't ask for once. Go."

"*Chobadeige,*" I said despairingly, and went out.

The rest of my grandmother's house had a strange unused smell. She kept the curtains drawn in the front room, to prevent the carpet fading, and it seemed, more than any room I have ever known, to be inhabited by its silent furniture. There was a large mahogany sideboard near the door, backed by a huge mirror which vibrated gently when you entered the room. At each end of the sideboard, in great vulgar vases, were the plastic flowers which my grandmother washed in soapy water once a year. Faded orchids, daffodils, distended tulips

44

with black preternatural stamens. In the dim room their jungle still-
ness frightened me.

I made swiftly for the biscuit tin and listened to my mother
and grandmother shouting on the other side of the wall.

"Don't you tell me how to raise my own son!"

"Someone has to tell you, sometime!"

"Why don't you mind your own bloody business!"

My grandmother's biscuits were always perfectly fresh. I ate
them quickly: three, four, five.

"So what if she's a *shiksa*! Better a nice *shiksa* than some *Yid-
dishe* bitch!"

Unbelievably, the sounds of a scuffle.

"You let me see my son!"

They are at the kitchen door. Something falls. I put my head
out.

My grandmother is standing in the kitchen doorway with
arms and legs akimbo, barring my mother's access to the hall. And
my mother is trying to push her way through, vigorously, but not too
vigorously: she has not forgotten that her opponent is old and frail.

She sees me and stops her shameless performance. My grandmother also turns her head.

"Get back in there," she commands, and the door slams shut
on them both.

But I linger in the hall, listening to the argument continue,
more softly now, more muffled. I go to the foot of the stairs and
look up.

My brother is up there, in the bedroom with the new carpet
where I sometimes sleep over. It has a high stiff bed with a white
candlewick eiderdown. My brother is lying on the bed, ill, damaged,
destroyed.

I go quietly up the stairs, and for the first time in my life I
feel nervous about meeting my brother. The bedroom door is closed.
I knock slightly. He says, "Who is it?"

"It's me."

No answer. Nervously, I open the door.

He is sitting on the edge of the bed with his back to me, apparently gazing out of the window. I walk round the bed and look at him. He does not look at me.

His face is red and crumpled, a torn face. Flushed with tears and beer. He stares out of the window.

"They're fighting about me, aren't they?" he says.

"Yes."

"What are they fighting about?"

"Granny won't let Mum come up and see you."

He smiles then. "Good old Gran." He bites his lip. Then the tears spill over. The tentative face collapses.

"Oh, God," he says. "I loved her. I really loved her."

My brother begins to sob and shake. I put my hand on his shoulder and I do not know what to say.

※

That summer he left home and went to London. I suppose he went to London. Where else was he likely to go?

When my grandmother died, our parents tried to contact him without success. So he did not attend the funeral. My mother cried a lot. She said she had never appreciated her properly.

We emptied my grandmother's house of all her possessions. All the furniture, the crystal, the carpets went to the sale room. And we found bottles everywhere: in the cupboards, under the bed, under the stairs. Always the same bottle: Irish cream liqueur.

When I entered the pantry with a cardboard box to empty it, I was knocked backwards by the familiar smell. It suddenly seemed to me as if the pantry was my grandmother.

※

We never emigrated, of course. The least inconvenient moment never quite arrived. Finally I reached that crucial stage in my education, which was their best excuse for staying put.

They must have felt some bewildered pleasure, to have such an academic daughter.

Meanwhile my mother drove me to youth groups and parties,

and nagged me to attend social evenings and date boys and go to the disco at the Judean Club, from which I returned in tears.

For she thought she had learnt one thing from her experience with my brother: that youth must have its fling.

They both continued to attend the Hebrew Circle. And my mother became an active fundraiser for the JNF. (Flowers of the Negev. Together we will make the desert bloom.)

My father is old now, he sits in the corner and he is no longer a well man. He sits in the corner with his dreams scattered around him like a drunk with his empty bottles.

⁊⋆

I have gone to London myself now and I sometimes visit them. I do not tell them much about my life.

It is pretty certain that I will never introduce them to Abigail. Nice Jewish girl as she is, I do not think she will fulfil their expectations. And I couldn't bear to see that grimace on my mother's face, the same grimace which crossed it when I showed her my first poem.

I am trying to find my brother. I don't hold out much hope. He has probably changed his name by now.

DEBORAH SEEKS HER BROTHER REUBEN LAST
SEEN SUMMER OF '78. PLEASE CONTACT.

Reuben: *Reu-ben*: See, we have a son!

Yes. I think he has probably changed his name.

It is a shame, because I think we could be of some use to each other. I would like to say the things to him that I didn't say back then. I'd like to tell him what I should have told him that Sunday afternoon I touched his shoulder. I was too young to know anything then. Now I know.

Dr Stein

On Sundays we sometimes visited Dr Stein. He lived with his wife in a frigid bungalow on the edge of the city. There was a door with a small chime; there was a hallway smelling of disinfectant. We were shown into a hushed lounge like a funeral parlour. Mrs Stein would bring us cold tea in dusty china cups embellished with the months of the year. She always took February. She perched on the edge of her chair, a dark dried woman with hair as short as a man's, and complained about the weather or the water supply or the lack of buses. We never left early; we always stayed late. We sat over endless drinks as night fell and the single bar of the electric heater burned uselessly against the glacial air, and Mrs Stein drew the curtains over the barren outlook one could hardly call a view. So I abandoned myself to those void Sunday afternoons of childhood which give us our first taste of futility and make us long for death.

Dr Stein was a psychiatrist, an opinionated man; but, having retired, he was no longer paid for his opinions. For hours he held forth on strikes, the state of education, the meaninglessness of Henry Moore. He resembled a petty Freud without genius, a man chiselled in the granite of his disappointments. He was strangely generous. He gave us his Rubinstein records because he hated them, and disposed of his tickets to Pinter like so many football cards. Occasionally he forgot himself and let slip an observation of such humanity that the room in which we sat seemed blessed.

During his harangues I would seek distraction in the textbooks which filled, lugubriously, the shelves beneath hideous pictures and steel ornaments resembling instruments of torture: *On Dreams and Dreaming* and *Models of Madness*; *Genes and Destiny*, *The Lost Childhood* and *Aberrant Sexual Behaviour*. I imagined Dr Stein creeping down in his pyjamas to consult the books at midnight, poring over them in the small hours with a glass of milk. They seemed totems of the strange mental world he must inhabit; though my ideas were shattered when I slipped one volume from its place and found it, in this immaculate household, furred with dust. Nevertheless, I thought, their mystical contents must long since have been absorbed into the involuted mind of Dr Stein, which I imagined as a kind of labyrinth hung with cobwebbed tapestries, strewn with the lumber of dead and elaborate theories: the faded wisdom of a lifetime's reading I could not hope to emulate.

I asked to borrow books and he acquiesced, in the careless shrugging way of one who has finished with them. All books, it seemed, were now beneath his notice. He knew everything; they could tell him nothing.

"Religion is an invention of the devil," said Dr Stein. "Sex is the opium of the people."

My mother protested with a nervous, smiling irony. Afterwards, in the car, she would make statements. "He's a bitter man," she would say, "but he has his reasons." Or, "He sees too clearly. He's the victim of his own brilliance."

Somehow I was always tricked into visiting Dr Stein. We would drop in after walking in the park; we would buy bagels and make a detour past his house. Not that, so far as Dr Stein was concerned, I existed much. Apart from the exchange of books (which, despite his contempt, he insisted be returned in good condition) we never spoke. He never knew that I had failed to make it past the second chapter of *Models of Madness*, or that *Genes and Destiny* had defeated me. He never guessed, perhaps, the mixture of awe and hatred with which I regarded him.

Nor am I certain why my mother took me there, unless it was to witness the impact of a suffering too deep to mention, which we had guiltily escaped, and the poison of which she felt it necessary to drink by proxy over and over again. There were no fresh flowers in the house, but a bouquet of grey teazles stood on the mantel near where his wife picked at her meagre tapestry, as though they alone could survive the toxic air.

I am convinced she went there for this reason also: in order to conduct a particular argument she had no hope of winning. Each visit was another round in the relentless boxing match between herself and Dr Stein. Tempers grew heated; voices were raised. Dr Stein used language my mother should not have wanted me to hear. And while his wife sat wordlessly unstitching a mistake in her needlepoint, the smallest of grimaces distorted her bloodless mouth.

"Everybody is to blame!" Dr Stein insisted; and repeated, "*Everybody—is—to—blame.*"

But how long, in fact, did we go on visiting Dr Stein? And how many times was I made to sit, unconsciously absorbing fallout from his vast hatred? It cannot have been so often, it cannot have been so long. Indeed, I sometimes wonder whether there was really only one visit, so interminable in its yawning boredom that memory cannot keep it whole.

And if this is so, if there really was only one visit, it must have lasted hours, hours in which we never ate, in which we barely moved, except perhaps to pass a photograph, inspect a painting hung above the fire: a painting, now that I recall it, of many archways one inside another. And now it comes back to me that Mrs Stein did once get up and open a pair of double doors, which led into a music room, a room with a step, on which there stood a Bechstein grand piano. And I remember how she ran a loving hand across it, though there was no question of her playing: in fact I am certain that she could not play.

They must have been fierce music lovers, but which music precisely did they love? Was it Beethoven, Bartók, Brahms? I cannot match any suitable composer to those distant afternoons, though I do believe that once, when my mother was choosing a record, the doctor moved aggressively in his chair and growled, "No bloody Shostakovitch!"

Really, I knew so very little about them. One didn't listen in those days and one did not ask. I can describe them merely: his square black glasses and the permanent pipe depending from a silver beard; the large cheap wristwatch and the sculptor's hands. She had perhaps been a dancer in her younger days, her brittle body still producing its trained formal movements; and I could see him, in our absence, tucking into meat and two veg, while she nibbled at a piece of toast, as though absorbing by natural right all nourishment their marriage had to offer.

But if I had asked questions, if I had known the bare outlines of their history, would that explain the secret of their strange alliance, this marriage without apparent sentiment or affection, which had, one might have said, a stone at its heart? There was a total desolation in the gesture she ran over the piano, the same gesture with which I saw her—with which I still see her—close the curtains on the lifeless view.

But I knew nothing. I can hardly disentangle dreams and memory, for I did quite often dream of Dr Stein. Like Freud's Wolf Boy I opened my window to find a dozen doctors hanging, great moons in the wintry night; nor can I be certain where the dreams ended and the afternoons began. Did he lecture me once with venomous contempt, reducing me to tears by his tirade? Did his great hands turn the pages of my secret diary, laughing as they went? The images are so vivid I wonder, sometimes, if a part of me is not still trapped in that eternal visit and whether, in dreams too deep to remember, I endure its airless tedium every night.

For I was nothing in the eyes of Dr Stein. I was worse than nothing: I was just a child. And being a child I knew instinctively how much he hated children. Yet my presence there cannot have been an accident. They needed, after all, an audience for their argument. Looking back now, I cannot help the notion that I was the whole motive for their meetings, that I was, in fact, a kind of experiment on which he and my mother were secretly at work.

"Television is an invention of the devil," said Dr Stein. "Democracy is the opium of the people."

My mother said: "You could learn a very great deal, you know, from Dr Stein."

But I never had the courage to ask. I put back *Dreams and Dreaming* and my hand hovered over *Aberrant Sexual Behaviour*. But I picked up *The Myth of Sisyphus* instead. Pencilled inside the front cover were the words: "Unreadable and not worth reading."

"I'd like to borrow this," I said.

"Hum! You can keep that one," said Dr Stein.

I watched Mrs Stein rise to draw the curtains (how fragile she was! it was amazing she didn't crumple like an autumn leaf) and linger a moment, as though waiting for someone to appear.

(According to Dr Stein, God did not exist. His atheism, my mother held, though justified, was the source of much of his unhappiness. But Dr Stein denied the existence of happiness.)

Mrs Stein drew the curtain with a gesture of despair.

Strangely, I always remember our farewell. We are standing in the bright hallway; the door is open on the frozen dark. My mother and Dr Stein have had their quarrel again: she wants to leave in dudgeon, but he won't let her. The quarrel continues. The hall is filling with icy air, and Mrs Stein cringes like a bit of blackened twisted root. I shiver, clutching my book. Will we never leave? My mother is pulling away. And then Dr Stein takes hold of my mother's hand.

"You must never part quarrelling from anyone you care about," he says. "You don't know if you'll get the opportunity to make it up."

Suddenly the room in which we stand seems blessed. And I know that in that moment my mother forgave him, hugged him, left the house with tears running down her face; and that she drove home purged, satisfied, having got what she came for, having got what she always came for.

"He's a bitter man," she stated, wiping her eyes, "but he has his reasons." And a little after, "He sees too clearly. He's the victim of his own brilliance."

Then I would sit in silence, mystified; and I would uncoil the great rope of boredom and resentment slowly from my head, and vow never to be tricked into visiting him again.

But we never did visit again; although I do recall the time my mother asked me to wait outside while she went in to see him where he sat, sceptically awaiting death. It was a bright summer's afternoon, and when she emerged in half an hour or so her eyes were red-rimmed; I believe I saw him standing for a moment at the picture window.

But that is a very long time ago, and if I were to go back now I doubt if I could even find the right bungalow. The trees will be taller, the bushes more mature; the lookout will not be quite so bleak, and I would not in any case discover Dr and Mrs Stein, who must both be dead, who must both assuredly be dead; in fact I would not be surprised if most of the people who knew them are now dead. They survive, perhaps, in a few snapshots with nothing written on the back, apart from which even their appearance must have been forgotten. Even my own memories are hazy, partial, more emblematic than actual; they are not flattering to Dr Stein. But they are more resonant perhaps than those of most people, who did not encounter him when they were children, who escaped his company unscathed, and who do not bear forever the marks of a malign influence.

Uncle Oswald

Why do the family always ask about Uncle Oswald? For years and years I have had nothing to do with him. They should understand that by now; yet they always ask: "And do you ever see anything of Uncle Oswald?" No, I reply, I never see him now. They shake their heads. "It's a shame," they say. "And he's your mother's only living relative. You should see him. Why don't you see him any more?" Then I am obliged to repeat the story.

I don't like telling it. It makes me uncomfortable. Not that I feel guilty: it was all his fault. But it doesn't show me up in a good light, all the same. I can't help reading in their faces, as I talk, a certain tight-lipped disapproval. I can tell they're not convinced by my protestations of innocence, least of all by my assurances that I have no wish to see Uncle Oswald in any case, that I am happier to have him out of my life.

They cluck and shake their heads without understanding. "Still," they murmur, "you ought to get in touch. He must be—how old now? Whatever, he isn't getting any younger." I don't need reminding, and as I drive back up north I am forced to utter aloud the retorts

I can't make to their faces. After all, they're related to him too, in a fashion. Why the hell don't they get in touch?

꙰

I am blessed with a large family—that is, on my father's side. My father was a remarkable man: a visionary, scientist, inventor. His relatives are all more or less remarkable. I love visiting them. They open doors in the mind, stimulate the intellect, and amaze the imagination with their ideas. It's a shame we live at opposite ends of the country.

I will never understand what my father saw in my mother, whose only remarkable act was to marry him. I am not saying she did not have a strong personality. She most certainly did. But she was in no way original, unusual or strange. In fact she was quite dull compared to him.

I think my father's family feel the same, though they would be far too polite to say so. They were as fond of her as I was, and miss her likewise; but I can tell, from certain hints they drop, from certain bitter comments, that they don't think she was quite good enough for him. He was a brilliant man who never fulfilled his potential: for this they blame her, as I suppose I do too.

Physically they were also very different: my father the classic intellectual, tall, thin and stooped, with bald patch and steel-rimmed spectacles; my mother the sensualist, short, broad, sporting the thickest calves I have ever seen and a truly Amazonian head of hair. As for myself, the product of this unlikely union, I am delighted to say I have inherited my father's characteristics in the main, with one notable exception: my hair is long, wild and voluminous, and, like my mother's, a flaming banshee red.

꙰

I traced my family tree once: through my father's side, of course. Londoners, back to the eighteenth century. Scholars, bibliophiles. One was a court physician. I know everything there is to be known about my father's ancestors, but about my mother's I know hardly anything at all.

They came from Poland: I've gleaned that much. Polish peasants or tinkers. Once—I think it was the day my grandmother died—we sat in Uncle Oswald's kitchen and found her birthplace on the map. I can still see his podgy finger pointing, but I can't for the life of me remember the name of the shtetl.

Anyway, there must have been a family quarrel, because they never communicated with their Polish relatives. Then, after the war, it was too late. My grandparents were the only survivors of two large families. Ada and Oswald were the sole representatives of their generation. It must have been a lonely feeling, like being washed up on an island after a huge shipwreck; and the island was England, of course. I have been thinking about that a lot recently. I imagine my mother and uncle washed up on the shores of England, two children clinging together. Everyone acknowledges that they were unusually close.

⁊

I have a photograph, it must have been taken during the war. They are both in uniform, smiling, their cheeks pressed together. It's a nice picture, a studio portrait. They look young and attractive. That is not how I remember them.

The way I remember it, they were both enormous, but Uncle Oswald was even more enormous than my mother. He filled rooms. I mean not just actually but metaphysically: he had a personality which filled rooms.

Bumptious, lumbering, gluttonous, vain, ugly man! How I used to shrink into corners when he (literally) darkened the door; how I used to dread his falsely velvet voice—his velour voice—demanding a kiss and a hug. He smelt of tobacco and whiskey and sawdust from the factory where he was boss, and when he pressed me to his gigantic belly I felt revulsion running in every vein. It was a lying embrace on both sides, mine and his: a manifestation of true family feeling.

I did not hate Uncle Oswald then. I merely disliked him. I disliked his waistcoat with the pretentious watchguard, his Jaguar with the walnut panelling. I disliked his fat laugh and his way of smoking a cigar, the tip of his tongue protruding. I recoiled in the simple

61

way of children, the way they recoil from a spider or a slug, but all my suspicions were confirmed the day my father murmured in my ear, "That's a pompous blighter, that one."

From then on my father and I entered a secret, unspoken alliance, an alliance of the Franks against the Finkels; intellect against trade; refinement against vulgarity. We were Franks. He was a Finkel. She? She would have liked to be a Frank, but she couldn't help it. Her ancestry was too powerful. She was Finkel through and through.

⸙

My uncle was jealous of my father. I state it baldly now: I did not know it at the time. As children, subliminally, we know things which only come home to us in adulthood with a sudden shock of recognition. It's part of growing up. I must have been twenty-odd when I first realised he was jealous. A weird shudder passed over me, like a snake shedding its skin.

Naturally, there was no contest. My parents were a devoted couple. Infatuated, the family say. That is their explanation for the strange alliance: "He was infatuated with her."

But Uncle Oswald never showed a proper respect for my father. He thought he was a weakling, a puny intellectual. This although my father ran a reasonably successful business. He never missed an opportunity to take him down a bit.

I remember, for example, the time my father demonstrated the Shoematic. It was his latest and best invention. Like all good inventions, it had an almost comic simplicity. A set of adjustable brushes surrounded a small platform. On the platform was a rotating belt. The shoe—still attached to one's foot—was placed on the belt, and merely by moving it back and forth, was effectively polished, buffed and cleaned.

My father, with the intent and quiet pride of the inventor, showed Uncle Oswald the mechanism: how the movement of the belt operated a series of rollers, which caused the brushes to rotate; how the transference of energy from one piece of the mechanism to the next reduced the effort required on the part of the user. He mentioned how it saved him having to strain his bad back and arthritic shoulder, how three pairs of shoes could be cleaned in the time it normally took to polish one. Closing it up, he displayed again the simple beauty of the casing, cunningly assembled from an old brass coal-box.

"So what did he do," the family ask, with that air of scepticism which always seems to colour our conversations about Uncle Oswald, "what did he say that was so terrible?"

He didn't say anything. He laughed. He laughed as though the Shoematic were the most amusing thing he had ever seen.

"And that's so terrible?" they shrug, for they are all inventors, accustomed to ridicule, and all as tough as old boots. But I remember the look of mortification in my father's eyes, and I knew I hated Uncle Oswald then.

⸭

There is a type of family quarrel, it is called the *brogez*. It is the kind of quarrel which occurs only in families or between close friends: people who know each other well enough to behave without any semblance of maturity. The kind of quarrel which took place between Saul and David or Sleeping Beauty's mother and the wicked fairy (who was really her unmarried sister). The term is both nominal and adjectival: Saul was *brogez* with David, and threw a spear at him, and tried to kill him; the queen and the fairy had a *brogez*, and Beauty pricked her finger and slept for a hundred years.

In general, the origins of the *brogez* must be as trivial as possible: a word ill-chosen or an invitation overlooked. The psychological origins, of course, are always Freudian in their complexity, and in both respects the *brogez* between my mother and her brother fulfilled all the criteria.

My mother invited Uncle Oswald to our Passover meal; Uncle Oswald declined, and went to a dinner at his club. Both the fact of his refusal and the manner of it stung her. He was offhand and contemptuous. To her it was not only a dismissal of his heritage but also a snub to my father, who would lead the service.

The unspoken message from Oswald to Ada was: I won't play second fiddle, and I'll jettison our past, too.

63

The unspoken reply from Ada to Oswald was: If I'm asked to choose, my loyalties lie with my husband and not with you.

They did not speak to each other for a long time.

Then my father died. One month later, after a rancorous absence of three years, Uncle Oswald re-entered our lives.

I was sitting quietly in my bedroom, reading Asimov. There was a knock at the door. My mother appeared, looking like a fat Bette Davis, with red rims to her eyes. She threw me a half-mournful, half-admonishing look, and in came Uncle Oswald, bigger than ever, truly gargantuan in fact; the slicked-back hair the same, the waistcoat and watchguard the same. The floorboards creaked as he entered. No-one could have looked more incongruous in my delicate bedroom with its lace curtains, its glass menagerie. He held out his arms and said in his velour voice, "Come and give your uncle a hug."

I did it for her. I hugged him.

※

After that Uncle Oswald came round for dinner every Friday, fitting us into the schedule which accommodated his ex-wife on Tuesdays and his ex-girlfriend on Thursdays, the woman he lived with on weekends and Monday nights at his club. This left Wednesday as the only night of the week when he had to cook for himself: on Wednesdays he ate fish and chips at the office.

Uncle Oswald had done well for himself since we were last in touch. He now had a three-year-old Jaguar with electric windows and a Rolex which could dive up to a depth of twenty metres. His jerry-built villa was filled with bad china and reproduction antiques. He also possessed the first home computer I ever saw. By moving a joystick and pressing a button one could send a white dot bouncing back and forth over a line on the television screen, and they called it tennis.

Soon after the reconciliation he took us out to dinner at a steakhouse where he addressed the waiter as George and George responded with a barely perceptible shudder. He ordered soup, sirloin and profiteroles, and a bottle of moderately-priced wine which he tasted with all the pretension of a fake connoisseur.

He would never marry again, he said. Marriage was a business contract, and he had no desire to go into partnership. Why put himself under obligations when he already had all the benefits? My mother remarked quietly that there was such a thing as emotional commitment. Uncle Oswald scoffed. He didn't know about emotions: he wasn't sure what they were. But altogether too much fuss was made about them, especially by women.

It was how they gained a stranglehold, he said.

My mother looked pale and tearful, and I could tell she was offended on behalf of her thirty-year marriage, which had been stable and loving and had ended so recently in bereavement; but Uncle Oswald stuffed his mouth with sirloin, he was impervious, he began to talk about my father. Why had he gone into gadgets? he wondered. He'd never met a man less suited.

My mother asked what Uncle Oswald meant.

"Well, let's face it," he replied, with the geniality of one who could afford to be generous to his rival now that he was dead, "he tried his best. But he was five-thumbed, bless him."

I thought of the hundred little improvements my father had made in our house, the mended locks and switches, the carved picture-frames, the gleaming Shoematic which still graced our porch. I could not believe my mother would let this slander pass. But she said nothing. She just wiped away a tear and dug into her surf-and-turf, and as she consumed it I was Hamlet, betrayed by the mother with the uncle: the lone and vengeful champion of my father's memory.

❧

Each Friday night, after the food and wine, they would retire to the lounge and watch television while I sat in my room, brooding. For my mother's sake, I would be polite during dinner. I did not make cutting remarks when Uncle Oswald showed off his latest gewgaws—calculators, pagers, musical gizmos, always, of course, the most expensive, top-of-the-range, only-the-best-will-do—but nor did I gratify him by paying them much attention. Up in my room I soliloquised and sulked, while they, heavy with good things, talked about old times, the stock market, the power of the unions. They had resumed a closeness whose roots were laid long before I was born, and which I had no hope of severing.

On Sunday afternoons I tagged along with my mother to his tacky villa, and was fed thin omelettes by Doreen, a tired, kind-looking woman whom he had seduced at the age of twenty and who now sat waiting for the marriage he had always promised without ever setting a date. Doreen ushered me to the bedroom, where sitting on the unmade bed with its sweaty nylon sheets, she showed me the bracelets he had given her, the thick gold chains, the rings. She described the choker she was having altered at the shop, set with amethysts and opals. "Ooh, it's a magnificent piece," she breathed, her breath smelling of hunger and acetone, "a really splendid piece." I watched her and wondered what she saw in him, what they all saw in him. Whether it was his natural ebullience, his aphrodisiac bulk, his sheer self-love, they were caught in a ritual of complicity no less than the drones which service the fat queen bee.

As for Uncle Oswald, he was under no illusions as to my feelings for him. One evening he appeared at my bedroom door and said, "I used to come here to see you and your mother; now I only come to see your mother." I tested the blade of these words; they didn't hurt me. Later I overheard them talking in the lounge. "It's a difficult age," my mother argued. "She's her father's daughter," Uncle Oswald disagreed. He couldn't have paid me a greater compliment; and we both knew what it meant. In the war for my mother's affections it would be a fight to the death.

※

The family are shocked by my colourful language; they don't believe me. How can I explain that that is literally what it was, that it was like murder, that nothing can atone for what happened?

"So they had a tiff, a silly argument. What about? He wouldn't give her a lift to the hospital? Is that a reason for a full-scale *brogez?*"

But he already knew she was dying.

"All the same, you should have phoned him. She would have wanted you to phone him."

But she didn't. I asked her. She said, "I never think of him."

"She didn't mean it. You should have phoned."

Yes. I should have phoned. But I didn't, and she died unreconciled. He never came to the funeral. That was the last I saw of Uncle Oswald.

❧

Years have passed. I've grown up. I'm my own person. I run my own business. People say I have a head for business. They also tell me to stay away from hammers and circular saws. Is that the Finkel side of me or the Frank? Am I a Frank or a Finkel? Sometimes I think I should change my name to Frinkel.

I don't like it when I read about genetic blueprints. About how genes are laid down in the foetus, some from the mother, some from the father. How are they measured out, how are they chosen? Can we be more like one parent than the other? Can't we dispense with father or mother? Is there no escape from our heritage, our unwanted traits, our betraying banshee hair?

❧

I did as they asked. A dozen years too late, I finally called Uncle Oswald.

But he was no longer on the telephone. The tacky villa had been sold. At last I managed to contact Doreen, who told me that since the business went down they had been living at the Golden Acres trailer park.

"Ooh, but it's a magnificent trailer," she enthused, "a really splendid trailer."

So I drove out to Golden Acres, where it seemed there were no trailers large enough to contain a man of Uncle Oswald's bulk and personality, but I found him sitting on the steps of a gleaming white-and-silver Elddis named Shangri-La. He had aged: all the robust rolls of flesh had sagged, as though they could support their own weight no longer, and the contours of his face had fallen.

"Hello, Oswald," I said.

Doreen was standing in the entrance, clutching a dishcloth.

She hadn't changed a bit. "She's come to see you, Oswald. Isn't that nice?"

"I've come to say sorry," I said.

Uncle Oswald lifted his enormous mass from the step where it was planted, slowly, like cargo being raised by cable. I thought of his body then as a gigantic sack in which our ancestors and all our history were held.

Uncle Oswald said, "I don't need your sorry," and went indoors.

That was it, then: I wouldn't see him again. I would have to do without his forgiveness, and now it had been refused I realised how much I wanted it.

I turned to go. A damp dishcloth touched my arm.

"Don't take any notice!" Doreen whispered. She smelt of parma violets, and close up I saw all the lines of waiting etched onto her twenty-year-old face. "He doesn't mean it. That's just him. Come on in and have a cup of tea."

❧

Why do I continue to visit him? Not for the pleasure of his company, that's certain. We cordially loathe each other. Politically we are poles apart. Yet each Friday night, in the flimsy trailer smelling of chip oil and adorned with tassels, I eat Fray Bentos pies and drink flat warm cola, and listen to the tirades of my Uncle Oswald.

The family is pleased, of course. And I am glad to have exonerated myself in their eyes. "How is your Uncle Oswald?" they ask now, and I can answer truthfully, "The same as ever."

For I cannot deny—and it's a source of some disquiet—that while he remains monumentally the same, I have begun to detect more and more similarities in myself to him. It may not be much—a phrase here, a gesture there—but each time it pulls me up short, and then I have to acknowledge: I am present in Uncle Oswald; Uncle Oswald is present in me.

But I wouldn't allow these sentimental considerations to influence me, and while I can honestly say that I no longer hate him, I can't really pretend to have forgiven him either; nor has he forgiven

68

me. That much is evident from the things we withhold. A few weeks ago I asked, as casually as possible, if he would point out my grandmother's shtetl on the map; he claimed never to have known it. Last Friday he mentioned a certain photograph, of himself and my mother, taken during the war; I denied all knowledge. I doubt if he will ask again. He's stubborn, and until he softens I shall certainly not repeat my request for the name of the shtetl, which will in all probability die with him.

Mrs Rubin and
her Daughter

T here would be no plant stall that year at the Blue and White bazaar. Mrs Rubin was dead, that vivacious lady. After a long illness, she had finally succumbed; everyone wondered what would now become of her daughter.

Not that she would be short of a penny or two. For the past twenty years the two of them had rattled around like pinballs in the big house, without any visible means of support. Julia had never worked; she had come back from Nottingham with some useless degree and sponged off her mother; the father, who dealt in *shmattes*, had been dead for decades. One could only assume it was all in gilts, stocks, trusts, offshore funds, securities.

Of course, she might have to share it. There were rumours of other daughters somewhere, a son, never seen, probably excommunicated. But Mrs Rubin was a strong-minded woman. It was more than possible she had cut them out of her will.

In any case, that was not the point at issue. For it was difficult to imagine Julia existing without her mother, or for that matter, Mrs Rubin without her daughter. They were always together. If Julia had been a paid companion she could not have stuck to her role more assiduously. Now her mother was gone, what on earth would she do with herself?

The women of the Ladies' Guild tutted and sighed over the sweet sacramental wine and dry fingers of cake, and congratulated themselves on having done much better with their own daughters. Their own daughters were lawyers in London, wives and mothers in Jerusalem. Poor Julia Rubin was unmarriageable and unemployable. But what did they know.

⊰

After her husband's death Mrs Rubin's conscience smote her and she turned religious. She refused to have pork in the house and took to writing God with a dash in the middle. She also insisted on attending synagogue on a Saturday morning. It was all as much for her children's sake as her own, for she began to feel they would never marry within the faith unless she set a good example; however, it was too late. Julia was the only one still young enough to be compliant.

The experiment, like the purchase of the large house, seemed doomed to failure. Mrs Rubin confessed privately (after the first confession it was no longer private, but soon became generally known) that she had bought it in order to tempt young suitors for her daughters. They would come for tea, play tennis, walk in the rose arbour and surrender to the heady blend of intelligence, wealth and beauty.

And the house was lovely, after all: a paradise. It stood in the heart of trees, at the head of a rolling lawn, beyond a winding drive from which the unwary visitor caught his first glimpse framed by an arch of syringar. It was a suburban Manderley. It had a tennis court and swimming pool, six bedrooms, three bathrooms and four toilets including one for the gardener. Not bad at all for a fortune built on *shmates*.

But the suitors did not come, or if they did they were unsuitable. They were ugly or stupid or raucous or shy. Once one of the more spirited sisters brought a bevy of gentile boys to the house: they were handsome and lively, ate pounds of cake and had Mrs Rubin in fits of laughter. It all seemed to go very well, but when they had left

Mrs Rubin turned to her daughter and said, "I would appreciate it, Marcia, if you didn't invite that sort of boy again."

Marcia was in no doubt as to what her mother meant by "that sort of boy."

One way or another Mrs Rubin was disappointed by all her children. The son was never spoken of, his crime having rendered him unmentionable. The daughters in turn ran off and did inappropriate things. At last only Julia was left and the martyred mother lived in constant expectation of a final betrayal.

"Go on, you'll turn out just like your sisters," was the bitter threat, repeated at the least sign of recalcitrance.

But Julia was determined not to turn out like her sisters. She loved her mother very much, and wanted to be good for her. When she had finished her uneventful degree (two nearly-boyfriends, one French kiss, long hours in the library) she thought of her mother, widowed and alone, still waiting for suitors in the great white elephant of a house. She was afraid of the world, and wanted nothing more than to go back home and keep her mother company. And Mrs Rubin, despite misgivings, let her do just that.

※

Mother and daughter lived quietly together. They did not leave the great big house. It was ridiculous really, just for the two of them, but they loved it. Julia did all the cleaning. It took her an entire day—Wednesday—and she did the upstairs and downstairs on alternate weeks. They got and lost gardeners like there was no tomorrow, and the farthest reaches of the garden were a wilderness, but Mrs Rubin's greenhouse was her pride and joy. She grew geraniums from cuttings and brilliants from seed, and her tomatoes were an annual event. Each year she carried a selection to the Blue and White bazaar, to help raise money for the State of Israel. Julia assisted: she sat three or four feet behind the stall and read a book.

No suitors came to the house, it is true: Julia had no tennis partner, and the tennis court was slowly growing over with weeds. But they were not reclusive for all that. Mrs Rubin was too active and vibrant a woman to cut herself off from the world. She attended auction sales and book-signings where she would meet old friends and gossip. She played the stock market and dined regularly with her accountant. Julia was the more reserved. She would not have social-ised at all if her mother had not insisted she make an effort and help out with the Jewish Youth. This she endured for three weeks until Mrs Gould observed that she seemed frightened of the children, and kindly suggested she might be happier with the elderly instead.

Nor was it quite true to say that Julia had never worked. There were five days spent in a solicitor's office, from which she returned every evening in tears, until Mrs Rubin felt it her duty to pay a visit and ask why they were persecuting her daughter. This was an impor-tant failure, one which Julia felt it necessary to hug to her breast and, in low moods, stab herself with.

People found her unnerving; if they had stopped to analyse it, they might have said it was because she had the eyes of a frightened deer. Not many people have observed the eyes of a frightened deer; nevertheless, that is how they might have described Julia's. Some gained the impression, on a first meeting, that she was a deaf-mute. At dinner parties she sat very quiet and still, while her mother laughed her descending arpeggio laugh.

Every Saturday morning they appeared among the sparse con-gregation in the ladies' gallery. The daughter was small, dark brown and mousy; the mother large, like her house, and swathed in volu-minous dresses. She had Spanish eyes.

After the service they joined the women of the Ladies' Guild for kiddush over wine and cake. Mrs Rubin flirted with old Mr Bogdan-ski and the rabbi. The women of the Ladies' Guild pressed Julia to take jobs in hairdressing, pedicure, be an Avon lady.

"She doesn't need a job," Mrs Rubin squashed them. "She's perfectly happy at home."

"She might at least sell tupperware," Mrs Cohen muttered.

They were not consistently religious. The synagogue stood on the same street as their house: it was also the road into town, and on Saturdays Julia was obliged to duck down as they swished past. They liked to eat out, and even at home they would sometimes consume prawns from a paper plate. Mrs Rubin had a fondness for the *St. Matthew Passion* and Handel's *Messiah*. She played them loudly on the radio-cassette, singing along in her erratic soprano:

> *For he is like a ref-i-i-i-ner's fire,*
> *A ref-i-i-i-ner's fire,*
> *A ref-i-i-i-ner's fire,*

Julia sometimes joining in with the Hallelujah chorus.

In the evenings they read aloud to each other. Mrs Rubin liked literature; her daughter worshipped it. They read Hardy, Dickens and Shakespeare (Mrs Rubin made a formidable Lady Macbeth), sighed over the natural descriptions and stumbled over the references to Jews, which leapt out at them like brigands on unexpected pages, making them wince: 'liver of blaspheming Jew', 'you Jew', 'villainous-looking and repulsive Jew', 'you're nothing but a lot of Jews'; 'Sir, even dogs have daylight, and we pay'.

Then they momentarily despised the writer, were alienated and repatriated in a flash, pressed on, admiring and despising, and forgot the literary mugging until next time.

When they were tired, around ten, they went to bed: to the same double bed Mrs Rubin used to share with her husband. They had their own ensuite facilities and when they had made use of them they got down side by side—Mrs Rubin on the left where she had always slept, her daughter on the right—kissed each other on the lips and went to sleep. Julia did possess her own boudoir, the former maid's quarters, at the far end of the corridor. But it was a good hundred yards away, beyond numerous closed doors and abandoned bathrooms, and she had not slept there for a very long time now.

☙

That was how the years went by. The trees grew taller around the big house; the water in the swimming pool a little greener and more stagnant.

Then one spring afternoon a young man walked up the drive with a book in his hand. He stopped a moment under the arch of syringar, arrested perhaps by its strong perfume, and received the mandatory view of Manderley beyond the rhododendrons.

Julia was writing on the front lawn. She did not see him at first. She was sitting on a camp stool with her back to the drive, writing a story. She had hair down to her waist and wore a pinafore, and looked about sixteen years old.

The young man asked her to excuse him. She started and covered the writing with her hand. Her eyes, which had been calm and intent, took on the expression of a frightened deer.

"I'm sorry to disturb you. I believe you left your book behind. At the bazaar." He drawled his words as though mocking her. The book, held in a stranger's hands, did not seem to be hers, and she accepted it hesitantly.

"Do you really find you can concentrate on poetry," he went on, "in a place like that? Or do you just carry it for show?"

She stared at him. He added, "Personally, I find Keats too effusive. But I do like that line in *Sleep and Poetry*—what is it?—'Life is the rose's hope while yet unblown.'"

By now Mrs Rubin was advancing down the lawn, her smock ballooning round her.

"Daniel Foster-Levy," he said quickly, and held out a hand.

He was a solicitor with a prestigious firm, and a recent arrival in the neighbourhood. Over tea in the conservatory (Mrs Rubin got out the blue service and a Zermansky's cake in his honour) it emerged that his parents lived in St. John's Wood, that he had been at Oxford, that he had achieved a first in History before switching to Law. With manicured nails Mrs Rubin caressed her jaw.

"Foster-Levy," she ruminated. "Would that be Foster as in Finkelstein?"

"No," he answered smiling, "that would be Foster as in Foster."

They ran through the list of mutual acquaintances, discussed schools and colleges and even a little politics, touched on the stock market and the theatre, and Julia, while she sat in silence stroking the back of her neck, could tell her mother approved; and when he had driven away in a black Mercedes convertible (discreetly parked in the street) her mother said, "He must have money of his own: he didn't buy that car out of his pay packet" and she knew that the suitor had finally arrived, the prince who must cut his way through the thicket to the castle and rescue her from her slumber.

҉

Two days later he was back again. On Friday night he was invited to dinner, and the following week there were tickets to the theatre.

Before setting off for town in the black convertible they took a tour of the garden. It was a balmy evening; Julia wore heels and a blue lace mantilla which, she discovered at the last minute, the moths had got into.

She showed him the broken down tennis court, the abandoned rockery and the weed-filled swimming pool. Beyond the pool, the greenhouse was a jungle of foliage, great strong tomato plants hung with ripening fruit. They stopped to contemplate it.

"Are they yours?"

"Oh no, they're Mummy's: they're her pride and joy."

"Do you think she'd notice if I stole a couple?"

"Oh, yes! She's very protective of them."

"Better not, then." He added, with unexpected rudeness, "Your mother reminds me of a marquee."

Julia did not answer. Blushing, she led him back to the conservatory.

The following Sunday Daniel pointed her out to his friend in the high street.

"That's Julia Rubin," his friend said.

"Yes. She's a nice girl. A bit shy, though."

His friend raised an eyebrow. "Girl! How old do you think she is?"

He shrugged. "About twenty-five."

"She's thirty-seven."

He looked again, and seemed to catch her glance. They both looked away again quickly. "What a strange woman," he murmured. Then he fixed his gaze on the nearest window display.

҉

79

Daniel Foster-Levy dropped by at Manderley. Mrs Rubin was arranging flowers in the kitchen. He wondered if he might ask her something.

"It's rather an awkward question. You'll think me terribly rude."

Mrs Rubin was certain she wouldn't.

"It's quite impertinent really, but I can't help myself. I have to ask it."

Mrs Rubin wished he would.

A pause. Mrs Rubin trims her gypsophila. The pieces fall softly: snip, snip, snip.

"The truth is, I've fallen in love with your house. I wondered if there was any possibility you would consider selling it."

Mrs Rubin has finished arranging her roses. She turns to him; she wears a smile like ice. All her perfect teeth—her own perfect teeth, and she is seventy-three—gleam between her parted lips.

"I suppose you think it is a little large for us?"

"Well, put it this way: it would make a marvellous family home."

A smile like a butcher's knife.

"I take it you are intending to provide one!"

Um, yes: as a matter of fact Mr Daniel Foster-Levy was engaged to be married. "Well," Mrs Rubin exclaimed, "congratulations!" And they laughed together, for she was a woman of unassailable dignity. "I tell you what," she said, "I'm a businesswoman, after all. I wouldn't turn down a decent offer. You name a figure and I'll consider it."

Mr Foster-Levy was about to name his price, but she forestalled him. "Not here in the kitchen," she said. "You go and consult your financial advisers. Send me a letter; we'll do this thing properly."

Three days later a letter arrived from Daniel Foster-Levy. Mrs Rubin read it, smiled, and filed it at the back of her davenport.

She told her daughter he wouldn't be visiting again. "After all," said Mrs Rubin, "Foster-Levy! What sort of a name is that? It's obvious he's only half Jewish."

❧

So the gates closed again on Mrs Rubin and her daughter. Of the last few years there is little to tell.

For a while Julia moved out of her mother's bedroom and returned to her own with its sprigged curtains and pre-Raphaelite posters. She thought it was time she developed some independence.

Then one Saturday when Mrs Rubin was driving the Volvo into town she complained that the accelerator wasn't working. Julia looked under the steering column. "Your foot," she said wearily, "isn't on the pedal."

Her mother had lost all sensation down her right hand side.

When she came home from the hospital she was clumsy and slow and couldn't speak properly: she looked at her daughter and said, "I'm Quasimodo." Nevertheless she made her painful way to the greenhouse, where the withered carcases of tomato plants were waiting to greet her.

"It isn't the end of the world," Julia muttered.

Her mother said, "I might not have another chance to plant tomatoes!"

She lived for a year. They spent it like young lovers, holding hands over restaurant tables, listening to music by candlelight. Julia even returned to her mother's bedroom.

Three weeks before her death Mrs Rubin went to Sainsbury's and bought a large piece of smoked bacon from the delicatessen counter. She considered she had settled her score with God.

She died in the Catholic hospice. On her arrival the matron bent over her and said, "Hello, Sylvia. My name is Sister Borgia."

Mrs Rubin let out a long, soft, wheezy laugh. She had always had an excellent sense of humour.

❧

After the funeral Julia sat in the conservatory and thought about her mother. The conservatory smelt musty; there were dead leaves on the carpet. She was thinking how strange it was that her mother, who was so vivaciously a Jew, should die among nuns.

That was the last that was seen of her. Not much later she left the area. The house was sold and demolished; a new estate was put up on the site.

Perhaps she went to London or Jerusalem, or Sydney, Australia; or Timbuctoo. Her mother had left her well provided for. She could surely go anywhere she wanted.

Someone said they had seen her in Southend one Sunday, shopping for bagels. Looking peaky and unwashed, they said, and much older. Personally I don't think it was her. I see her somewhere else entirely, sitting in a white room whose windows open onto the Mediterranean. There is a small dog at her feet and, at her side, a bowl of red roses. Her eyes are calm and intent. She is writing a story.

An Italian Child

I have an Italian child.

High in the hills west of Florence, off the road to Viareggio, next to the chapel of San Stefano, in a villa hung with jasmine and a pergola of roses where they eat in summer: that is where my son lives. A villa with large dark rooms, green shutters, a view of olive trees and the distant Apennines; a garden with fir trees and rabbit hutches and a barking dog. In the morning the cockerel crows at dawn, all day the voices call him, Jacopo, Jacopo, he crosses the field on his long brown legs; he rides the tractor with Umberto and collects small red plums in a basket for the noon meal. He is dark, he is thin, he does not resemble me: he has a sensitive mouth. His eyes are accustomed to the sun, his long eyebrow touches his temple. My boy will be seven tomorrow; this is all I know.

❧

Mrs Webster places the fax on my table and says: You'll have to do this one by teatime. It's urgent. That is how she speaks to me. She says the minimum, as though, if she allowed herself to say more, we might be drawn into the rapids of conversation.

We're well suited. I don't want to talk. Later, we will take tea at our desks, eat a ginger biscuit each, pore over our translations. Sometimes, on the telephone, I hear her speak French. It is incongruous, like drinking cold claret.

The number seven bus rides past my window in a sluice of rain, and another twenty minutes have gone by. They will be taking their siesta now at San Stefano. The high bedrooms with their enormous wardrobes, their great laundry-presses, stand dark and still behind the closed shutters. He lies, a check of sunlight on his cheek, in a sea of tangled sheets and toys. His limbs are like sticks: I have seen the photographs.

I know what the afternoons are like at San Stefano, how Maria always rises first, makes English tea because she likes it that way, sweeps a few leaves from under the pergola. While I, who never learnt how to sleep in the daytime, spent the hours thumbing books in the study, gilded editions of Hardy and James with their light signature, E. Matteotti. Under the pergola, holding her teacup in both hands, Maria told me: There are two people in Emanuella, a princess and a peasant. Sometimes she likes to be a princess, sometimes she plays at being a peasant.

Yes, I said, but me she expects always to be a prince.

Well, I know my own daughter, she said, and you know your wife. But how to keep her satisfied, that's always the question. We had many conversations there, among the roses, while Emanuella was sleeping.

And later when the others emerged, one by one, from the darkened bedrooms, Umberto carrying a disarranged La Stampa, Emanuella winding her hair into a knot, we sat aside, Maria and I, in our collusion, the taste of secrets still in our mouths. And I watched my wife a little guiltily as she reached into the cupboard for the water-jug, knowing I had talked of private things she would resent, the intimacies, problems of our marriage.

Mrs Webster is sipping her PG Tips now, eating her biscuit with an intense, abstracted look. Her husband, I believe, is a professor of semiotics. Perhaps his obsession with symbols has driven her to silence. Perhaps they communicate with each other by looks and signs, by semaphore.

Only once did she notice the photograph standing in a corner of my desk. It's my son, I told her. Oh, really? And on an impulse, forgetting herself, she picked it up. He doesn't look like you, she said. No, I agreed, he doesn't. He always looked Italian, like his mother.

⁂

Another bus passes and the next but one, the five-fifty, will be mine. This summer we haven't had a summer. It has rained, I think, every weekend, with sunshine only on alternate Mondays. You are a different person in the heat. Your body frees itself. You become aware of your shoulders particularly, as the bravest, most sensuous part of yourself.

In San Stefano we were different people. Strangers. Seven summers visiting, we never made love in San Stefano.

Jacopo was conceived in an English winter, in front of a two-bar electric heater, in a third floor flat off the Kilburn High Road, in complete happiness. We dreamed of impossible lifestyles: six months here and six months there, if it was a boy we would call him Jacopo, if a girl Francesca. We ate granary bread and hard pale English tomatoes; she wore my lumpy sweater. Circling her knees with her long, foreign hands, she talked authoritatively of dual culture, of the privilege of bilingualism.

For you and me it is different, she said, one of us will always be a stranger. But he will be at home in both places. He will be truly English, truly Italian.

(Christmas, Roehampton, my mother's house: Emanuella turning over the pudding on her plate and murmuring, mortified, I can't eat this! My incomprehension, as I settled back in my usual chair, of the way she perched rigidly, like a typist, on the edge of hers. My barely concealed irritation.)

He won't be English or Italian, I answered. He will be ours. We will be his homeland.

(Easter, Lucca, the cathedral: in front of the holy Cross she lit

87

a taper, pulled her shawl over her head and genuflected. Done for my benefit, to remind me how easily she could fall out of my arms and back into belief. Her profile, pale and still as a saint's, said: These are the things which are mine and not yours. Now you are the exile.)

Jacopo, Mrs Webster repeats. That's a lovely name. But no-one could pronounce it, and the children laughed. They're calling me Pinocchio, he cried, they say I've got a long nose. I stroked his smooth hair (dark: Emanuella's hair, not mine) and thought, We should only give our children ordinary names. We should not afflict them with beautiful names which will be made ridiculous.

❦

'In rapidly changing markets, flexibility is essential and a streamlined decision-making process allows fund managers to respond positively and quickly to events. Furthermore,—' I glance at my watch. One day they will have computer programmes to do what I do. I always wanted to translate great literature. But how many people are privileged to do that? One or two, perhaps, in a generation. Sometimes, at home, I still dip into *I Promessi Sposi*.

I wonder what tomes Mrs Webster has explored in the original French. Some Molière, maybe; a bit of Racine. The standard texts she probably still keeps from her student days. It is difficult to imagine her tackling anything more racy, through her half-glasses.

They say, of course, that something is always lost in translation. That may be true; but something else is gained. I love the strangeness in translated English: the spareness or lushness which breathes through it, spareness, perhaps, if it is from the Italian; lushness if it is from the Spanish. English grows, for once, exotic, sprouting fruit you'd never find in a Surrey garden.

Conversation is a different matter. It is easier to tell lies in a foreign language. Which is surely why so many people pray in Latin.

Day is darkening prematurely, the air intensifying for another flush of rain. My husband is meeting me, Mrs Webster says; would you lock up? She has her umbrella at the ready, the coat with the orange check which she wears summer and winter. She has already lost the bit of tan with which she returned from two weeks in Provence.

And so she rushes off. We have never spoken about it, but she knows I have nobody to rush for. English fashion, she avoids asking personal questions: nothing is any of her business. Even when she picked up the photograph and was dying to know, she politely refrained from inquiring about the boy's mother.

Emanuella always accused me of not talking enough. So like a man, she said. Getting words out of you is like getting blood out of a stone. But so far as I remember we were always talking: it was the language which let us down. And then, in San Stefano, it was the body language. Maria noticed. She doesn't address you, she said. She doesn't look at you. Something is wrong. As if we could attempt to cover the miles of frozen waste between us by handing the spaghetti. And so I had to tell Maria: You're right: we cannot communicate.

I double-lock the blue door with its faded brass fittings and step out into the rain (a true Englishman never forgets his umbrella, and I raise mine like a black ensign). Ms. Matteotti, you were always so intense: an overdose of literature and politics had killed your sense of humour. When you frowned your whole face aged a generation.

You certainly did not remember your umbrella that day you ran out into the Kilburn High Road, wanting to be free, tears and mascara and hair streaming down your face, your dark dress clinging. Thrusting me off as though I were the warden of some institution you had escaped; while all I could think of was Jacopo, abandoned in the flat, and the fear that you might dash under the next bus. Don't touch me! you shrieked, playing both peasant and princess at the same time, the rain trickling into your Cartier shoes, and I thought, stupidly: I don't suppose we are going to the party now; I will have to telephone and make our excuses.

I step back as the number seven slooshes in to the stop, carefully close the wings of my umbrella and climb aboard. The interior of the bus smells like the changing room at the squash courts, but for a moment, seated safely here, I feel an intense rightness, almost happiness.

How easily one can slip into the habit of being alone again, of eating toast at midnight, wearing socks in bed, putting off tedious errands until tomorrow. We can manage without each other, after all. I knew that when you clutched at Jacopo, your hair dripping, and flung the towel back as though I could give you nothing else worth having.

⁂

My place is small, and faces north: beneath my window a graveyard stretches to a belt of trees; it makes a sort of garden. Rain casts itself against the windows like a sad relentless comforter.

I plug the kettle in and reach for a tin of soup. At San Stefano now they will be bringing dinner under the pergola, setting plain white plates on the flowered oilcloth, a jug, a basket of bread. Voices come from the kitchen, Italian fragments, *Ma no, e poi, capito*, the dog pads in and out on slow paws, following the dishes with its hopeful muzzle; a slow trail of smoke rises to the stars. Jacopo is playing with his cousin: the two boys circle the house like greyhounds. Hidden in the barn is his birthday bicycle.

They say the Tuscans are descended from the Etruscans, that they have even identified a Tuscan gene. How would it be, I wonder, if my Jacopo looked like me, if, among the dark-haired and almond-eyed children there was one fair flabby child called Jack who couldn't stand the sun? How would his mother feel when she looked at him? Would she always remember, would she love him in the same way? But he is not flabby and fair, he is dark and thin as a spider: his aunt breaks a piece of bread in her jewelled fingers and says, But have you felt his arms? There is nothing there, not even any muscle.

I carry my tray of soup to the lounge and without more ado switch on the television, the colour and noise of which throw an instant blanket over loneliness. These are the things one does not admit to: that one cannot live without the television, that it stays on all the time, that it is a wrench to turn it off, last thing at night, and suffer the equally instant silence and darkness. I will watch anything except gameshows: news, hospital dramas, comedy thrillers, hospital comedy drama thrillers with topical themes—anything to dull the brain and ward off solitude. It is nearly two years, and when two years are up we will be made official, stamped void, our decade together acknowledged a legal error.

90

Maria writes to me that she is well and happy, and maybe hopes I will derive some selfless pleasure from the knowledge. Sometimes, perhaps, she thinks of me, with the nostalgia of complete detachment. I am glad she is well; I'm not surprised she is happy. Who can blame her, everyone said when they heard she had gone back, isn't it very lovely there, and after all, it is the place where she belongs. I wanted to answer that we belong together, that a husband and wife should be their own country, that one should not abandon the other. But I did not say so, for these notions of loyalty are not popular. The kingdom of love is not a fascist state, even under the rule of marriage. All citizens retain the right of free passage, and may, if they so wish, revoke their citizenship.

I have an Italian child. A child who has forgotten his English, who speaks only Italian. A child who if he wrote me letters would begin 'Mio caro papa,' but he never writes. He is running in the garden now at San Stefano, catching fireflies; it is late and he should be in bed. The fireflies hang in the darkness like Christmas lights; the jasmine whose flowers, they say, are the holy stars which fell at the birth of Christ, stands heavy with scent near where the adults talk. My grandmother used to say that once you have children you are never alone in the world, there is something of them in you, of you in them: you have thrown in your lot with existence, planted your stake in the future. Somewhere at San Stefano my flesh and blood is running under the stars. He catches the languid fireflies and traps them beneath a jar in the kitchen. When he comes down in the morning there will be money.

Waiting for Rain

After several days of rainless heat, the northern town of Binley begins to take on the characteristics of a middle eastern souk. The smell of rotting vegetables seeps from alleys, gutters turn vile and viscous, pavements are splashed with spit. Tattered awnings are rigged up; dogs wander. In the bus station, the smell of tar and petrol mingles with another, distinctly foreign odour: that of burning metal. The bus queue reels in the heatwave from a passing bus. By the ticket office, the flower bed is completely bare, the earth dried into hard grey lumps. It looks as if nothing has ever grown there, as if nothing could ever grow there. The effort would be too great. One begins to excuse the neglect, and to understand the mentality of hot countries.

※

Three or four patients sit in the dentist's waiting room: a mother controlling her child, a man reading a magazine, a young woman with her hands in her lap. Mr Cowan flutters into the surgery like a piece of blown paper. "It's going to be another scorcher," he tells Miss Louth, the dental nurse.

The young woman is the first patient. A wisdom tooth is giving her pain. She drops her handbag on the floor and climbs awkwardly into the chair.

The dentist reads her teeth and Miss Louth makes notes. His probe gently and relentlessly investigates. The young woman knows now that she is nothing but a mouth, and lying on this chair the rest of her body is ready to drop out of existence.

But before it has a chance to do so, she must stand up and walk downstairs for an x-ray. The tooth has got to come out.

She leaves the building in tears.

※

The woman whose body is ready to drop out of existence on the dentist's chair is twenty-two years old. Her name is Greta. The main thing about Greta is that she has come into some money and is living on it for a while. She has no occupation, nor plans to have any; she has, in fact, no plans.

The necessity of making appointments with the dentist a week, two weeks in advance, is distressing to her. It presumes a future existence, with dates, times and destinations. She wishes to exist only in the present. But her tooth is giving her a great deal of pain, it cannot be ignored. It has made the present peculiarly incisive and unbearable. She has been trapped into making an appointment. That, and the painful prospect of having the tooth removed, cause her to cry as she leaves the surgery.

She takes the short walk home, knowing that from now until the time of the next appointment she will be in limbo, waiting. It had been her intention to remove all possible islands of expectation, except for that last, inevitable one. Now a tooth has robbed her of her peace of mind.

※

This gritty town, labyrinth of asphalt and exhaust fumes, ferments strangely in the sun's heat. Tarmac softens. Stone burns. Even metal has transmuted into some brittle, unreliable substance.

The people, too, are going through a process of change. The

heat acts on them like a catalyst. For some it is a liberator, loosening their limbs and freeing them of conscience and inhibition. For others it is an oppressor, crushing them into dark corners of constraint and waiting. Crimes of recklessness increase during the time of drought. Doctors are entreated by streams of sleepless people.

The nights are as hot and airless as the days. The eyes of the town are open in the small hours. Mr Cowan drinks milk in his kitchen and reads a journal; Miss Louth lies in a cold bath and contemplates her naked body; our Greta sleeps the sleep of the just.

The drought has continued for seven weeks.

※

The treatment will cost about forty pounds. That is more than two pounds a year in lost interest. Should she skip a meal or two to make up for it? That is a false saving, for she will only eat more at the next meal; and our Greta loves her food. Besides, if she once uses the tactic as a money-saving device, she is liable to take it to extremes and starve herself to death.

She is filled with anxiety, not for the first time, as she sees the small island which is her money shrinking around her. Forty pounds here; two pounds fifty there; fragments washed off by the tide of necessity, never to return. Time and again, in meticulous calculations, she has balanced income against expenditure, only to find it falling just short. She must dip into her capital, in turn reducing the interest, and so on down the slippery slope.

She can economise no further: her life is already pared down to the essentials. She must somehow supplement her income. She decides to seek a job.

(If the personnel manager at the supermarket wonders about the origin of Greta's Mona Lisa smile, it is this: that money, which is freedom, can only be obtained by enslavement. Even Greta, who thought herself immovable, has compromised. She has agreed to chain herself to the till for fifteen hours a week in order to conserve what little freedom she can.)

Nothing comes free of charge, especially not money. Greta lost a mother to get hers. Others give up their health, their peace of mind, their dreams; most valuable of all, their time. Every life is mortgaged. Greta's is no different.

ঽ৵

It is hot in the supermarket. From where she sits she can see the light beating against the glass doors. Greta is one of those who are released by heat; she adores it; looks out of the doors with the eyes of a lion gazing through the bars of a cage. She is almost literally chained to the till, for she cannot leave it unless a supervisor comes with a little key, attached to a chain, and switches it off so that no-one can get at the money inside.

And now Greta discovers how dirty money really is. The coins are warm and greasy in her palm and the notes dusty and dry. By the end of the afternoon her hands are black from it, and up in the staff toilets she has to soap and rinse, soap and rinse to remove the metallic smell. Her mouth is full of money words, too: they are all she has spoken all day. When she eats the food tastes of money.

One of the supervisors is kind, the other is cruel. Once they have a disagreement about Greta's tea break: standing in front of her they argue about it. At last Greta is allowed to go.

The canteen is a dismal place with no windows. Everyone wears the blue uniform with the name badge and the emblem of the supermarket; Greta's is wrongly spelled. The name badges prevent people from introducing themselves.

The cruel supervisor sits opposite Greta as she drinks her coffee. Greta feels she should speak. She says, "There was some dispute about whether I should have a tea break?"

Immediately she regrets having referred to it. She has stepped out of line. The supervisor leans towards her and her heavy brows almost meet in the middle.

"There was no *dispute*," she says scornfully. A pause. She leans closer. Greta cannot quite make out what she says. It sounds like, "You don't know me, do you?" It sounds like a threat.

Greta hastily leaves the canteen.

More even than operating the till, Greta hates to sweep the floor. Her legs are feeble after long hot hours of sitting. She feels degraded.

98

Even the kind supervisor will mercilessly switch off the till when the store is quiet and ask her to "Give us a sweep." This reminds Greta that she is the lowest of the low. She is filled with slavish rebellion as she drives the tide of receipts and wrappers before her wide brush. She thinks of Spartacus, of Che Guevara. She will topple the system, she thinks with an inscrutable smile.

She watches the clock as it slowly peels off its hours. Every fifteen minutes make eighty pence. Fifteen minutes have never seemed so long.

❧

The heat has begun to take on a life of its own. It has acquired the nature of an epic: people are aware that they are living through something momentous. There is talk of standpipes, of the dry beds of reservoirs, of deaths.

Now it is as if there has never been a time before this drought, nor will there ever be an end. Even the cautious northerners have discarded their chunky clothes and step out, blinking, into the natural warmth. They walk in a new way. They no longer care. If a road has to be crossed, the cars will stop all right. And if it isn't done today it can be done tomorrow, for the days are endlessly long.

Everything that is sinister or threatening in the town is lured out like lizards from under rocks. This sort of weather gives people illusions. They imagine they can get away with anything. The night streets crawl with restless youths looking to prove themselves, even if it is only by breaking a window or scaling a wall. There is an imminence of chaos, the breakdown of structure, and then? State of emergency, looting, burning, rioting, the end of the world, and what does it matter? In this heat, what does anything matter?

❧

An elderly man with a shock of long white hair, a frayed waistcoat and an enormous paunch, always chooses her checkout for his groceries. He reads her name from the badge and teases her to know its origin. Her shyness only encourages him. Before long he greets her by name, like a friend.

She can tell from his basket that he lives alone: the box of eggs, the packet of biscuits, the sliced white bread. He does not take care of himself. He is a lonely eccentric, a sort of troglodyte. Perhaps he is drawn to her by their similarity.

Laughingly, she even tells him about her tooth. He is sympathetic. "I promise you it will not hurt," he says, in his threadbare, academic voice.

She has comforted herself that the extraction will not hurt, because of the anaesthetic, and that has given her a kind of courage during the limbo-time of waiting. The old man's promise cheers her. It is only when she is seating herself with fragile bravery on Mr Cowan's chair that she remembers: when the anaesthetic wears off, then it will begin to hurt. She regards the promise as a betrayal.

It is then that she resigns herself completely. Let everything be done to her. She thought that she had come here through choice, in order to be rid of pain, but in fact it was only a choice between one pain and another (and she has to pay for this!). Since it was not to be avoided, she may as well offer herself up to it entirely, without protest.

To Greta, pain is not a matter of degree. Once it starts, it may as well take over.

⁂

The supervisor with the heavy eyebrows is holding a till roll under Greta's nose. She runs it through her long, manicured fingers, stopping it every so often with an impatient tug.

"And here," she is saying, "you've sub-totalled again. And here—and here." She says in a voice like honey, "Why do you keep sub-totalling, Greta?"

It is only with great effort that Greta can get herself to speak. "I must have made some mistakes," she says indifferently.

The supervisor looks at her long and hard. Her mouth is set and there is a dangerous gleam in her eye. "Well, try to be more careful," she says at last. Her stilettos stab the floor as she struts away.

Down in the canteen one of the girls is crying and crying,

while a friend puts an arm round her and smokes a cigarette. Her sobs travel down the tables; people glance over curiously. The crying goes on and on, all the time Greta is drinking her coffee.

She sees that she cannot do even this most basic of jobs properly. She knows that she is making mistakes all the time, cheating customers, robbing the store. Besides, every moment is torture. Her dreams are filled with numbers, lists of prices, endless sub-totals.

Moreover, she has discovered another curious and alarming fact. Although she should now be managing to keep her finances on the level, it appears that the money in her account is dropping faster than ever. Increase of income brings increase of expenditure. The earnings from the supermarket are actually having a negative effect. She begins to realise, with creeping horror, that she is caught in a spiral from which there is no escape.

The girl in the blue uniform is still sobbing. Greta decides that she must quit her job.

꒰

Cracks are appearing in the square around the cenotaph; it is forbidden to water the withering roses. Air shimmers like cellophane over by the taxi stand where the Asian drivers linger and peel off, one at a time, in their shabby Toyotas. It could be Athens, Cairo, Delhi. It could be a desert shanty. The whole town could be a mirage and be gone tomorrow. It quivers on the edge of crisis, like a mirage.

Now people queue as a form of prayer, with buckets, at standpipes, at supermarket checkouts. (The price of bottled water has doubled.) They believe that if they queue patiently and in an orderly fashion nothing bad can happen to them. It reminds older people comfortingly of the war.

Every household has received a Government leaflet: Save and Survive: Getting through the Drought. On the front are two hands cupped protectively around a drop of water. Of course there is nothing sinister behind the absence of rain. Of course it will rain before long—but meanwhile, follow these simple rules…

The rules are repeated on posters and billboards all over the town. It really does remind one of a war.

❧

When he hears that she is leaving, her friend the troglodyte is genuinely sorry. He wants to know what she will do and where she is going. Greta, fearing his motives, is guarded and obscure. She smiles cheerfully as she says good-bye.

Two minutes later he is back with a bunch of flowers (they sell them from a bucket by the door). He thrusts them into her hand and, before she can speak, kisses her. His hair, waxy and unwashed, rubs against her cheek, and his stink is enveloping. The next moment he is gone.

Greta stares at her browning chrysanthemums, at once flattered and appalled.

"Do you know that man?" the supervisor asks.

Greta looks at her in bewilderment. She is not sure whether to answer yes or no.

"Only," the supervisor goes on confidentially, "it's not the first time he's bothered girls around here." She drops her voice. "I'd be careful if I were you. Don't encourage him. You know what I mean."

❧

The stitches in her gum have been removed and Greta is invited to pay her bill. But she is also invited to make another appointment. There may be more trouble: fillings, another wisdom tooth. Curious fact: once a dentist has you in his hooks, it is very difficult for him to let go. If he cannot make capital out of pain he will play on fear.

Greta firmly refuses. There will be no more islands of expectation. She is methodically dismantling her life. And this is not difficult to do: notice given on a bedsit, a discarded job, a building society account closed. The cheque is neatly folded in her pocket.

She is clean of everything now, except this money, which is her freedom. What will she do with it? She could buy a car. That is another form of freedom, only, like money, one which depreciates.

She could buy a plane ticket to—anywhere. She could take a ship or a train. She could buy a motorhome and travel round the country. She could buy herself clothes, luxuries, a further education. Schemes extravagant and absurd tumble through her mind, but she cannot choose one because it must be to the exclusion of all the others.

If her inheritance had never existed she would have been forced to make a life for herself. As it is, she is paralyzed. Dimly, she becomes aware that the money is not in fact her freedom but her prison.

≈

Though it should be autumn, nature too seems paralyzed, unable to progress. No wind strips the leaves from the trees and makes them dance; instead they drop with straight funereal slowness. Colour is bleached from the roses in the town square.

The people of the town stand in their queues and wait. And now their minds are full of bewilderment and suspicion: perhaps they have been betrayed or misled, perhaps they have been lied to and manipulated. But it must have been way back now, and anyway they are too tired to do anything about it. These are the people who stand meekly in their queues and hope.

In the heart of the town, which has become a Middle-Eastern souk, a shanty, a trembling mirage, others are ready for the conflagration. These have taken possession of the woven streets and created a zone. They are bound not by plans or schemes or networks of subversion but by anger.

There is a strange glow about the town at night, as if the lefto-ver heat of day is boiling off. The pavements are almost luminous; the beat of a walking boot creates weird reverberations. A glass shatters and a dustbin lid falls, and the aftershocks echo into every sleepless bedroom.

This is how the conflagration starts: a glass shatters and an alarm goes off, and a young man in a windcheater bearing the legend "Illinois 32" has broken into the supermarket. The alarm is ringing fiercely as his companions follow him in. They are past caring about an alarm, about punishment. They have a raging thirst to quench.

They are going for the bottled spring water. No, they are going for the wines and spirits. Illinois 32 screws the top off a litre bottle of whisky and pours it down his throat. The others follow suit: they snap the rings from beer cans, one pops the cork of a champagne bottle. Here is something to celebrate! Here is a party worth coming to, a birthday, a holiday, a festival all in one.

The ringing alarm casts a note of frenzy over the jubilation. Time is short. Drink! Drink as much as you can before it's taken away!

Illinois 32 smashes the neck from a bottle of ten-year-old brandy and pours it onto the floor. It sinks into the carpet which Greta once had to vacuum.

He signals to his friends, who, with bottles under their arms and in their pockets, step back and watch. A distant siren has joined the ringing of the alarm.

The young man strikes a match and drops it. At once, fires break out all over the town in an act of spontaneous combustion.

※

The people are tossed out of their houses and into the streets. Even Greta, sleeping the sleep of the just, has woken and joins them.

There is no time to put on more than a light summer dress. She cannot discover her shoes. Barefoot she runs out into the street, to watch the town on fire.

The building next to hers is burning; the surgery, the building society, the supermarket, burning. Now the roses in the town square are going up like paper; the cenotaph is circled by a ring of fire.

Some are already trying to escape. But the roads are black with people: their cars cannot get through. Horns, sirens, alarms: the town is screaming.

Greta ducks and bobs her way amongst the crowd. She cannot be looking for anyone. There is nobody in the town for whom she bears any concern.

She becomes aware of something immensely heavy in her pocket. Something is pulling at it like a lead weight. She puts her hand in her pocket and takes out a piece of folded paper.

It seems impossible that a piece of paper should weigh her

down so heavily. When she holds it between her thumb and forefinger it almost flutters away. Yet she is carrying nothing else.

Out of the corner of her eye, she spots the troglodyte.

His jacket is smoking, his face brushed with soot. Whether he has just been saved from the flames, or has been saving others, she cannot tell.

He is the one person in this town for whom she bears any concern. She approaches him and says, "I have a present for you."

Before he can answer she has pressed the folded cheque into his hand. At the same moment a knot of astounding panic tightens in her throat.

But she has given and is gone before he can say a word. As she pushes her way blindly through the crowd she thinks: I have just given my mother to a stranger.

❧

Our Greta has left the town behind. It is glowing in the valley beneath her. Slightly breathless, she is making the last ascent up a bank of brittle heath, without even a piece of folded paper to weigh her down.

At the top of the slope she halts, plucks the debris from her light summer dress and looks up. She has reached the reservoir.

On every side of it the moors open out, low, dark and treeless, edged with the steely light of dawn. The once dripping wilderness, slashed by becks and noisy with waterfalls, has become an arid desert hovering on the edge of ignition.

The deep crater that was the reservoir oozes mud and sticky pools. The retaining walls, once hidden beneath the water, stare like the hull of a beached ship. A vast puddle lurks in the centre of the basin, draining slowly away.

Here, once and for all, is the truth of the matter.

All along she has known that she would come to this place in the end. Here there is no escape, no shelter. Merciless dawn is rising. Evaporation will be almost immediate.

Deep in the heather she turns onto her back, her face to the sky. Somewhere in the distance she can hear thunder. But the sky is bright, hard, brilliantly blue, and holds no promise of rain.

Mr Applewick

M

r Applewick finished dinner early and drove out to see his client. He put on his brown check suit for the occasion.

The Metro was still gleaming. It barely came out of the garage these days. Business was slowing down, but he didn't mind. It left him more time to himself.

He glanced at his image in the rear view mirror. His face was very clean, very pink. The pale blue eyes stared back at him, magnified through the thick lenses like marbles in a glass of water. His silver hair stood up very short and harsh, and when he put a hand to the back of his head there was nothing but bristles. He disliked the slight heaviness around his lips, for he did not consider himself a sensual man, but in all respects—the tightly buttoned waistcoat, the severely knotted tie, the spotless trousers—he was refined and harsh. He had in fact, Mr Applewick noted with satisfaction, become what he really was.

His client lived only a short drive away, on the Moorcrofts. The address turned out to be one of those big, mock-Georgian houses without symmetry or grace, surrounded by hideous shrubs.

He walked up, as always, with deliberation and without hurry, and rang the bell.

A sulky child answered the door and was swiftly removed by its mother. She fussed Mr Applewick into the dining-room, steering his bulk around the draylon furniture and precarious knick-knacks, until they reached the object of attention.

Mr Applewick put down his attaché case and summed it up. It was a Broadwood, upright steel frame, walnut casing, probably made around 1910, after the firm had moved from Great Poulteney Street. The casing was in extremely good condition, polished to a high lustre which clashed with the oak veneer of the dining suite. It was remarkable how many people kept their pianos in the dining-room these days, where they wouldn't be a nuisance or interfere with the television.

He sat down, adjusted his seat and took possession of the instrument with a few chords. It was badly out of tune, some of the notes were sticking and strange resonances wheezed from within.

"It hasn't been played for a while," his client explained.

Mr Applewick stood up.

"If you would mind clearing the top," he said. She hastened to do so. Mr Applewick helped her, transferring the bric-à-brac to the table piece by piece. He had little respect for people who used their pianos as sideboards. The ornaments interfered with the resonance and even rattled when playing appassionata. But he removed them gently and would not have dreamed of showing his distaste, for he was a man of impeccable politeness.

He opened the top, put one knee on the piano stool and peered inside. The hammers needed refacing, the tapes replacing, it would want new check leathers and a general clean at least. Then, it was so long since it had been tuned that wires were liable to snap when the action was refitted.

He came off the piano stool.

"It was my mother's," the woman apologised. "I've never played it much, but now that Samantha's going to start lessons I thought we might as well—"

Involuntarily his eyes wandered to her hands. No indeed: no-one with nails that long could be a serious pianist. He glanced up. The sulky child was peering round the dining-room door, sucking its thumb and looking none too pleased at the prospect of learning to play the Broadwood.

Mr Applewick moved a hidden lever and the front of the piano came off. Mother and child started back in alarm.

"Oh! I didn't know you could do that," she said.

Mr Applewick struggled under the weight of the front panel.

"If I might put this against the wall there—" he gasped.

"Of course—sorry—" The woman scurried out of the way.

The piano tuner returned to his closer inspection of the interior, testing notes and examining the condition of the hammers and dampers. The inside was beautifully decorated with scrolls and leaves, now faded and dusty. There was a good deal of burnishing to be done.

"It will be a big job, an expensive job," he said at last. And he began to explain what needed doing.

"But is it worth it?" she wanted to know. "I mean—is it a good piano?"

"Oh yes," said Mr Applewick. "It's worth doing. I wouldn't suggest it otherwise." She did not know what a Broadwood was. He would have liked to abscond with the action.

"We'll do it, then," the woman compromised; and Mr Applewick opened his attaché case to reveal a gleaming array of tools, each lying in its own specially shaped well. He set to work removing the piano's action, taking each section out to the van, until the casing stood derelict and every footstep made a ghostly echo.

"I suggest you clean out the dust from there," Mr Applewick said matter-of-factly, indicating the filthy ledge where the keyboard had been. The woman's face looked exactly as though she had failed to vacuum under the bed. Very gently, Mr Applewick let down the lid, which sloped in now like lips do when the teeth are gone.

"I'll get in touch in about a fortnight," he said at the door, and gave the woman his card: *A.J. Applewick, Piano Tuning and Reconditioning. (Caterer to the Musical Profession)*.

❦

Mr Applewick took the action through to the workshop at the back of his house and set it up on the bench. The workshop was a single-storey extension built by his father, with a large window overlooking the garden. The light was going now, and he switched on the fluorescent strip, which drenched the white walls and threw everything—bench, shelves, trays, tools, Mr Applewick himself—into high relief. Nothing was out of place, and there was not a speck of dirt. The metal trays he had fixed to the walls himself were all neatly labelled: Clip Felt, Wedge Felt, Check Leather, Loops, Tapes. A sweeping brush stood in one corner: he always swept up immediately. His cutting board was clean, his knives sharp. He never ate or drank in the workshop.

Perhaps he took things to extremes, but his was a precise, clean craft and he had his father's standards to maintain. Every element of his drill had been ingrained before the age of twenty.

Once, a long time ago, he had stepped inside an artist's studio, and been horrified at the apparent chaos: the dirty palettes lying here and there, the used rags and unwashed brushes, the half-eaten cake and festering coffee cup. He felt that nothing refined or clean could be created in such a place; and true enough, the paintings turned out to be chaotic daubs, without recognisable form and content, without, even, any recognisable talent or skill. They just broke the rules, and Mr Applewick saw no benefit in that.

He should have waited till morning, but he had a sense of urgency about the Broadwood. It would be a big job. And he enjoyed working on it. He looked forward to seeing all the hammers fresh and firm, the springs responsive and the new tapes snapping back and forth. Even after forty years he had not lost that sense of achievement.

The first time he had finished a restoration entirely on his own he had hardly wanted to return the piano to its owner. He sat in the workshop, gazing at the fresh hammer felts which looked like the eyes on a peacock's tail, searching for any speck of dirt or adjustment still to be made, until his father came in smiling and said it was time to go. They had the Bedford then; the Moorcrofts hadn't even been built yet.

Mr Applewick went to the window and took a look at the sky.

It would be a clear night. Good. It was dark enough for the whole room to be reflected into the garden. His own face hung amongst the irises like a ghost.

He returned to the workbench, removed his heavy glasses and rubbed his eyes. Perhaps he was tired, after all, and should leave the job until morning. He laid the action face down and began unscrewing the hammers, placing them in a small box marked 'Hammers.'

A faint familiar odour of leather and glue hung in the workshop. He thought of his father, as he often did when he was at work because it often seemed to him that he was standing in his father's skin, performing his actions, wearing his expressions and even grunting the same grunts. They were of an age, now, too, and that thought gave him a little shiver.

They were both perfectionists, both of a scientific turn of mind, with a passion for order. Neither of them spoke much. In the workshop, talk consisted of, "Pass me the bushing now, please," "Set the glue on, would you?" "Steady, now, and lift!" They were always extremely polite to each other, as if in deference to the fine instruments on which they worked.

His father was religious. He believed that he had been given certain abilities by God, and no more. And so he taught his son a craftsman's pride in building pianos but a layman's humility in playing them. Mr Applewick knew he had no musical ability. He could produce the necessary chords for testing the piano's tone and tuning; perhaps a few commonplace songs. The Knight in his living room was barely ever opened.

As he unscrewed the hammers, he thought, This Broadwood is certainly a noble thing. Mozart and Handel had played at the Broadwoods' concert hall in Great Poulteney Street and Chopin had given his last London recital there. Mr Applewick did not care for Chopin. He admired Bach, Vivaldi and Handel. For him, elegance in music was everything. It stuck to the rules. Now that composers had broken the rules the result was chaos and it was certainly not music. Indeed it was not even composition.

Mr Applewick often wished that he had lived in a previous century, when life was altogether more elegant, manners more courteous and customs more ornate. Either that or in the future, which had its own endless possibilities; but he certainly didn't care for the shabby little place the world was now.

In the old days, his father had subscribed to a number of educational magazines in an effort to improve himself. He had inquired into the world with a sort of wide-eyed wonder, marvelling at the works of God and man. He had the enthusiasm of a child running loose in the Garden of Eden, knowing that God had made everything for his investigation and delight.

Mr Applewick was not religious and he knew that the garden was not only full of serpents but full of other people trampling on the flowers. He did not believe in God and he never had done, and secretly he despised his father for being so naive.

When he was eleven years old he had become interested in astronomy. He saved up his pocket money and with some help from his father he managed to buy himself a second-hand telescope, a three-inch refractor which was hardly better than a pair of powerful binoculars, but it was a start all the same. He went through the usual teething troubles, leaning out of the bedroom window with no mount, going out into the frozen garden in the middle of the night with his pyjamas on, trying to make sense of over-detailed star maps by the light of a torch. But gradually he had become proficient; he kept his equipment in the garden shed and worked from there, he bought a decent tripod mount and began to learn the skies. And the more he learned the less he was able to believe in God.

His father had the exactly opposite response. Mildly impressed by his son's new avenue of knowledge, he allowed himself to be initiated, patronised and introduced to the mysteries of the tube. The boy half hoped that when his father put his eye to the telescope, atheism would strike him like a revelation. Instead, Mr Applewick Senior adjusted his position, gazed long and silently, slowly panned the heavens and whispered with awe, "How many are Thy works, O Lord! In wisdom hast Thou made them all."

The son could not help himself: he snatched his father by the shoulder and grabbed the telescope with a look of fury. It was the only time he showed such anger, and it was the only time his father looked through the telescope.

❧

It had grown late. Mr Applewick got up, switched out the light and went into the kitchen to make himself a cup of tea. Night hung at all the windows; he went around drawing curtains while the kettle boiled. He would not do any more work on the Broadwood tonight. Automatically he reached for his quilted jacket from the back of the kitchen door and put it on, then took his cup of tea and a biscuit into the back garden.

Just behind the workshop was a run-off shed he had built himself. Inside was a sturdy five-inch refractor on a large tripod. It was Mr Applewick's observatory.

He pulled out a stool and balanced his cup and saucer on a nearby ledge, adjusted the telescope and began focusing it on Ursa Major. It was so cold that the bristles on the back of his head seemed to ripple. He smiled to himself. This was the moment of his reward: no-one could now enter the small circle which contained him and his telescope.

What he knew, what he had learned—not just the constellations and the planets, but the advent of meteor showers, the existence of distant galaxies, the positions and magnitudes of almost ten thousand stars—all this streamed within his blood like a kind of love, and revolved in his brain like a kind of hope. The limitless possibilities of the universe intoxicated him. He wished he could fast forward time and know what was to be discovered: the exploration of other worlds, the sun's death and Earth's destruction, the wonderful contraction of the universe into cosmic egg and big bang and cosmic egg, the pulsating of a universe reborn over and over again, as new, with no previous knowledge. He wanted to see it all! If there was a God, he imagined Him working with a piece of clay, moulding it into a universe, then rashly impacting it once again, never satisfied with His production. But there was no such God, for not even God could survive such cataclysm.

Because he was a scientist and a lover of detail, he kept careful diaries of his observations. He had several notebooks now, immaculately written, though he did not pretend to himself that they were of any great usefulness. The useful work an amateur could do now was negligible, he accepted that. He had once met another enthusiast who wore out his eyes in a nightly hunt for comets. He yearned to discover one and have it named after him. Mr Applewick thought the man conceited and absurd. One did not have to justify astronomy by sensationalising it.

He had, in fact, himself discovered a comet some while back. It was in the year his father died, so it was an unusual year in more ways than one. He had made his recordings conscientiously and written to the BAA. As it turned out, a mathematician had already computed its orbit and the comet was named after her instead, but whenever Mr Applewick looked it up in the Handbook he felt an affection towards it.

The practice of astronomy, which seems so broad-sweeping and expansive, is in fact a science of tiny details and pedantic calculations. In this sense it did not sit so uncomfortably with the restoration of pianos. As Mr Applewick measured and cut the leathers for his jacks, as he painstakingly glued each one in place, his nature was in harmony with his work. But in his mind he may well have been considering the primeval matter from which all things come, and the cosmic dust to which jacks, glue, leather and piano will ultimately return.

Whatever his thoughts just now, Mr Applewick made a sudden movement, caught the teacup with his elbow and sent it clattering onto the concrete floor of the shed. He straightened up; all his joints were stiff with cold, and his back ached. He picked up the broken pieces of the cup, laboriously wheeled back the shed and stumbled indoors.

※

The next day he was up before dawn. Standing in the kitchen he sipped his tea; he would make an early start.

This morning, more than usual, he felt how his clothes were a little too tight under the arms and around the crotch, and as he ran a comb through his minimum of hair he became transfixed by his own reflection. Strange and impassive, the magnified eyes stared back at him.

He was at his bench by six o'clock. That morning he dismantled the dampers and found that during cleaning he had mislaid the tray. It was large and difficult to lose, but he could not see it anywhere. He made a careful reconnaissance of all his work surfaces; he found the hammers and levers nestling quietly where he had placed them the night before. He started to look in unlikely places; sweat prickled under his arms and on the back of his neck. Then, just as he was about to lose his temper, he found the offending tray on the floor beneath his workbench, just where he was most likely to put his feet. He could not understand how he had done anything so stupid, and picked up the tray with something like hatred.

He selected those dampers which required re-covering and began to scrape off the old felts with a knife. He was still a little angry and cut away at the felt with some ferocity. The red backing would not detach itself from the wood of this damper, but instead of fetching some methylated spirits to loosen it, he vented his frustration on it with the knife. He cut himself, and blood deepened the redness of the felt.

Among his labelled drawers were those marked 'Clip,' 'Wedge,' 'Split Wedge' and 'Parallel.' These were the four types of felt used on damper heads. He bought them ready cut from the suppliers, and had only to glue them in place.

It was something peculiarly concordant with that day, that first day, that he opened the drawer marked 'Clip' to find wedge, and the drawer marked 'Wedge' to find it full of split. He said aloud, "Someone's been messing about in my workshop," but since it was obvious that the only person to have been in his workshop was himself, he choked on the final word and coughed.

He solved the problem very simply, by removing the labels from their metal frames and changing them round. Now all was in order once again. He took what he needed and returned to work.

He concentrated harder than usual during the glueing of the felts, checking several times that he was fixing the correct type to the correct head, ensuring that no glue dripped where it was not wanted. The day was getting on by the time he finished and he realised that he had not eaten. He would leave the dampers to dry and go and get a bite to eat.

It was odd, however, that despite having counted carefully, he now found that he had one wedge felt left over. He hunted the workbench and tray to see if there was a stray damper anywhere. But it seemed that he had accidentally brought over an extra felt, so he would just have to pop it in the drawer and go for some lunch.

Now he found that the drawer marked 'Wedge' contained clip; opening the drawer marked 'Split' he found it full of wedge. The Parallel drawer held split and the Clip drawer parallel—in fact, all the drawers were as they had been before someone had changed the labels round. Mr Applewick began to suspect some kind of jinx was on. He grew cunning. This time he changed the labels back stealthily, then made as if to walk away. Next he wheeled round and tore open the drawers, half-expecting to catch them in the act of transferring their contents. All were exactly as he had left them. He stared into them for a few moments, his eyes huge and watchful behind their thick glasses, then slowly pushed the drawers shut with his finger-tips. He left the room backwards, almost swaggering, and shouted aloud, as if to some unseen presence, "I'm going to finish this job if it's the last thing I do!"

He did no more work that day.

ᘘ

From that time on, battle was engaged. The glue pot would fall to the floor and need wiping up; he would cut a piece of bushing wrongly and it would tear out of true. He seemed unable to tie a knot in a piece of string or to smooth out a length of tape. Impatience brought more mistakes. He broke the head off a rusty screw when he tried to force it with his screwdriver, and scorched himself with the casting lamp when he was loosening the tail.

A few moments of peace came with the burnishing of the jacks. With a piece of check felt and some black lead, Mr Applewick felt once more in possession of his territory. He was making the Broadwood shine, and a burst of love passed through him. He was saving it from decay; he was saving himself from decay. In effect they were serving each other.

His nights he spent in observing the stars. He tried to imprint their discipline on his disordered brain. Yet it seemed to him that all the stars were speeding away from him at tremendous velocities, leaving him alone, a mere fragment of life circling a doomed sun.

This was strange, because the universe had always seemed a friendly place to him, with its rules and regulations. Only now, it began to seem rather impersonal, and for the first time in his life he felt lonely.

Back in the fifties, when the Russians launched Sputnik and cars had rocket fins, there had been a girl called Eileen who lent him science fiction and listened to Bach. They went to the pictures together and exchanged ideas on the future of the universe. At one time they had almost been engaged, but he had broken it off. He returned the books. He blotted out books, films and Eileen from his mind.

Mr Applewick had no memory of love.

He sat alone in the middle of the night with his telescope, his workshop and the Broadwood, and the stars were all racing away from him.

❧

Sixteen days later he was ready to return the action to its casing. Mr Applewick took a bath and put on a clean shirt. He fitted himself into his brown check suit and his shiny shoes. He felt sweet.

It was exactly six o'clock when he rang the bell of the asymmetric house.

"Ah! Mr Applewick. I'm so glad you've come to put the innards back in this thing. Every time you walk past it echoes as if it's got a ghost."

Mr Applewick got down to work. Not a sound came from the rest of the house. Not so much as a cup of tea appeared. When he began tuning, a dog started to howl somewhere in the distance, but that was all.

While he was tightening the strings one snapped with a sound like a bullet. Mr Applewick put a hand to his heart. No blood. A terror was growing inside him. When all was reassembled and tuned and he began to play, perhaps the Broadwood would produce a cacophony, a travesty of music, exposing the chaos within him? Perhaps he had botched the entire job, made a farrago of the Broadwood's insides, something that could never function?

As he sat down to play the regulation chords his fingers trembled. He closed his eyes. The chords rippled out. He worked his way up the scale. It was a beautiful instrument. He had restored it.

Mr Applewick began to play one of the tawdry songs which were the only pieces he knew. He longed to be able to draw something meaningful from the throat of the instrument.

Hearing the music, his client dared to re-enter the dining-room.

"That does sound good. What a difference!" She hovered behind him. "Are you all right?" For Mr Applewick looked ill.

Mr Applewick closed the top for the last time and invited his client to try it out.

"Oh—well—I don't think....!" She sat down stiffly and played a few wandering notes with one hand.

"Yes—oh, yes, that's fine. That's lovely, thank you." She got up quickly. "I suppose it'll want tuning every so often?"

"Well, regular tuning does retard deterioration of the action. You see—" He began to explain why, speaking slowly and using terms she did not understand.

"How often, then?" she asked impatiently.

Mr Applewick regarded the Broadwood with a mixture of sadness and affection.

"I wouldn't leave it longer than a year," he said at last.

༝

When Mr Applewick was found, cold in his bed, an examination of the house was made to rule out any possibility of accident or foul play.

The house was in a dirty state, and the soiled linen in the bathroom spilled over the floor. The kitchen sink was full of unwashed dishes and a thick odour of rotting vegetables hung about the downstairs rooms. The shelves held worn piano makers' manuals, bound copies of educational magazines and dusty piles of astronomical journals, star charts and calendars.

The workshop itself appeared to be the domain of an untidy and disorganised man: the floor and work surfaces were covered in odds and ends, tools lay scattered and dangerously concealed, drawers were torn half-open, their contents spilling onto the floor. Spiders had woven their webs in every corner, and the once beautiful felts and leathers were full of moth and mildew. All inside was confusion, chaos and decay; while outside in the overgrown garden, the run-off shed when pushed back revealed, rusted to its tripod, an old telescope with a broken lens.

Moonlight

After his death the house was found to be filled with peacock feathers. That is a superstition we no longer know. We would not be troubled by peacock feathers in the living room, in the hallway, arranged with sprigs of honesty in a Chinese vase. Peacock feathers in the bedroom would not disturb us. We have forgotten that they were once symbols of vainglory and the evil eye.

Nevertheless he kept them: deadly and beautiful, they lurked in forgotten corners of his studio with ammonites and conch shells and bits of pottery and broken glass, all the early tools of his trade. They gathered dust on the windowsill with myriad objects of study from the days when, walking with his wife, he would fill his pockets with bones and leaf skeletons; or when the children, knowing his obsession, would run indoors with fragments of oxidised mirror they had found in the garden; or when, transfixed by the refraction of light, he would stare at the bevelled glass in a chandelier.

He was a connoisseur of objects, a man in love with the objective world. This alone must have made it peculiarly difficult to die. He had squandered himself on items: on the chiffoniers and Flemish vases, on the buhl French timepiece and six grand Dutch marqueterie chairs, the wall plaque medallion of the King of the Belgians and the suit of armour, richly chased with shield, which fetched eighteen pounds at the auction after his death.

He was fifty-seven years old and perished of a painless cancer. And this is what we are told of his death: that he did not stop working, that ill and in debt, he remained at his work until he could stand no more, crawling upstairs finally on his hands and knees to bed, to the Persian brass bed with the silk hangings. That he sent away the priest, that his friend read Tennyson and Browning and sang Schubert's *Schlafe, Schlafe* at his bedside. That he laughed over Kipling's *Lord of the Elephant* in the small hours. That when his daughter saw the death in his face at dinner he told her to go and take her meal in the kitchen.

Of the mundane details which make up a man's dying only these fragments are left, for it was, after all, not exceptional, this death of a man of minor fame. In the course of time it might seem almost nothing: a burial plot in the city cemetery, a longer than average notice in the local newspaper; an auction sale and the vacant lease on a property his widow could not maintain. A bonfire of peacock feathers and spoiled canvas. And, naturally, the legend of his last words, whispered to his wife, but only alleged or attributed, a family tradition merely, and too theatrical perhaps to be believed: "No sun, no moon, no stars."

※

I do not know when I first became interested in him. Perhaps when I was still a young assistant, back in the Sixties. In the cellar storeroom of a provincial gallery, the curator pulled aside a canvas and showed me a suburban lane at twilight, a gothic mansion behind a wall; trees, carriage tracks; a lone female figure with a closed parasol.

I have never forgotten it. Yet that cannot have been the first time I saw one of his paintings. For the scene was indefinably familiar: like a place visited in childhood, like the road not taken.

Of course, I know now that he painted many of these, perhaps too many, perhaps dozens or scores of them: the lane bending either to the right or left, the sky cirrus or clear, by moonlight or sunset, always with the titles 'Golden Twilight,' 'Silver Moonlight,' 'Golden Light,' always with the same female figure moving away into a distance not spatial but temporal, away into the past. Is it any wonder that you sense you have been here before, when the artist evidently has so many times, so many times he might have painted it in his sleep, and the whole scene might only be a rendering of some troubling and recurrent dream?

But then I thought the painting was unique; I did not know that it was representative of a long and delicious trauma, only one of many lanes in a labyrinth where the artist had lost his way.

I do not know, even now, why he began to paint, down there on the canal amongst the engineering sheds, the gasworks and the wool-waste warehouses. Was he inspired by visits to the city art gallery? By engravings in the gentlemen's magazines? Perhaps he took his first enthusiasm to the house of John William Inchbold, the local landscapist. 'He was a delicate young man of about one-and-twenty, not much over five feet tall, and pale: my immediate impression was of a chronic consumptive. He told me he was presently working for the Railways, but that, notwithstanding the opposition of his parents, who were strict Nonconformists of the dourest kind (his mother had thrown his paints on the fire and turned the gas off in his room to stop him painting in the evenings), he was determined to become an Artist.'

That is the sort of account one can imagine, if any had been given. 'I asked him if he had had any formal training. None, he answered, but what his own observation of professional work had given him, and a few evening classes at the city art school. I gave him what encouragement I thought fit. In those days, you must remember, to embark on a career as painter was no longer quite the fool's errand it had once been: Art was increasingly in demand amongst the rising classes, and a competent Artist, who must once have earned his crust as a drawing-master or making woodcuts for the Library of Entertaining Knowledge, could sensibly dream, if not of wealth, then of a decent living. No longer a mere coach-painter or sign-painter, a face-painter or a hand-and-drapery painter, an Artist could, in a plum waistcoat, cut a figure in Society. Nevertheless, I was wary of nurturing such fantasies in a young man whose talents were as yet unproven.' And so on. But we do not know if he even visited Inchbold.

What do we know? That his mother kept a grocer's shop and his father was an ex-policeman. That he fell in love with his cousin at an early age. That he attended the Philosophical and Literary Society at Philosophical Hall and exhibited his first works at the Rifle Volunteers Bazaar. That a local bookseller agreed to display his canvases on condition they were not painted on Sundays.

It's a romance: by the time he was thirty he was earning £100 for an oil painting and £10 for watercolours but his figures were still atrocious. He moved uptown to the new villa district. Perhaps because he couldn't paint people he concentrated on landscape. It is said that the effect of landscape on him was so powerful as to make him ill. He travelled the country with his brother who was a salesman for a firm of nail-makers, which is curious since his paintings were as bright and hard as nails, his lake scenes dead as moths: exact and lifeless as a photograph.

He espoused Ruskin's 'morality of detail' and painted what he saw. His foregrounds were precise botanical studies. When he painted his wife 'at home' a mere ruck in the carpet became a challenge of technical skill. He perfected his figures, painting her in the garden, at the window, cutting camellias in the greenhouse. He had her pinned for ever in the airless beauty of the drawing-room, vacuous, laden with silks, listening to silent music; surrounded by cashmeres, china, peacock feathers.

Art made him a gentleman. He took up the lease on a fifteenth-century manor house and commissioned a gothic retreat overlooking the sea. He rented a studio in Chelsea and exhibited at the Royal Academy. He enjoyed friendships with Millais and Whistler. In his conservatory on the coast he grew vines, oleanders, anthuriums and other exotic plants from which he extracted pigments. He was regularly represented by the London dealers, Agnew and Tooth.

These are the relics of his golden years: the fob watch engraved with the Masonic symbol, the coromandel walking-stick with silver head. Elephant tusks; silk slippers embroidered with his monogram. All sorts of crystals. The skull of a monkey and a goblet said to have belonged to an ancient Chinese emperor.

⅌

I never had the talent to be an artist. That much was clear to me from the very first. There are some people who, for all that they can analyse a master's every brushmark, could never produce a stroke of genuine art.

My mother always told me to stick to what I was good at. "Words are your métier, Norman," she would say. "Words and discipline." She was pleased to see me do well, get a dull degree, a dull safe job and not go chasing after precarious fantasies, precarious lifestyles.

So I resigned myself early to pure analysis: a surgeon, dissecting genius I could never have.

"A real intellectual, our Norman is." It always gave me pleasure to make her proud. I know she watched with relish my progress from assistant to curator to director to academic hack. Climbing the greasy pole for which I was well suited, but never creating anything of my own. It pleased her to fantasise about my grand future. "Norman, Keeper of the Queen's Pictures." Mother was always something of a snob.

⅌

I have seen the house where he lived, like a mediaeval baron surrounded by fake armour and Roman pottery, in grim drawing rooms, in dark corridors hung with rugs. I have noted its dank walls in photographs, the high trees full of rooks. The plumbing was said to be deadly. In the narrow nursery three of his children died from fumes caused by a faulty sink outflow. The ex-actress hired to assist him pined with a slow TB.

He read Tennyson to her under the lilac trees while his wife sat in the mullioned window like the Lady of Shalott. When autumn came they fled to London, abandoning wife, children and his collection of claymores.

129

He painted the docks by moonlight and the prostitutes on London Bridge. Railway arches; gaslit fog. The flash of a match as a man bent to tend his pipe; omnibuses on the wet cobbles. A moonlit land loosing her ships into a black sea, lighting her flares. On the calm horizon a silver moon hung steady; in the still house his wife awaited his return. The actress assistant coughed into the darkness. They buried the dead children one by one.

What can we know now of the lost letters, the forgotten gossip, the hotel rooms hired under a pseudonym, the railway sleeper carriages booked for two? What of the secret notes, the rendezvous? Or the private diary, now dust and ashes, in which he recorded in the faintest of hands, 'Miss Neale died yesterday at Scarboro'?

(The official account: 'She was invaluable to me in the mix of paints and colours.')

I have seen the rose garden and the croquet lawn, the staircase down which you could drive a coach and four. I have seen the pictures taken before the demolition: the streaked walls, the boarded windows; the scutcheons salvaged for the city museum. The stone griffins lying in a sea of nettles and the neglected graveyard for the family cats and dogs.

※

There are times when I utterly despise my work: when I see the pointlessness of turning paintings into words. The art critic, like the music critic, reduces the irreducible to a heap of opinions.

Let me tell you what I feel when I stand before his pictures— before any pictures. It is a sort of despair. It is the sort of despair only Art engenders.

I have to struggle for interpretations. The airless drawing room with its dull woman represents the ennui of Victorian domestic life. The glade with primroses and a pretty stream expresses nostalgia for the rural idyll. The gaslit quay bristling with trams and horses idealises the city and casts a romantic sheen over the industrial revolution. Why did he start painting, why did he paint what he did? I don't know, I hunt for reasons. The philistine hunts for meaning in an act whose very performance is a cry for meaning.

I wonder whether I, too, could not have done as much, if I had only been blessed as he was with those Victorian virtues, the 'triumphant power of enthusiasm,' the 'divine faculty of work.' Perhaps then I should not be haunted by the unfinished pictures lurking in the cupboard, the dried and twisted tubes of raw umber and terre verte, Payne's grey and cadmium red; and by the bundled brushes, rounds and filberts, sable and bristle, stiff with disuse; and by the old palette with its record of many attempts.

⁂

The nature of the financial disaster which struck him in his mid-forties is not precisely known. A piece of misjudged generosity, perhaps; an unwise investment or a rash gamble. In any case, the London adventure ended. The seaside retreat had to be given up. He retired to the manor and painted to pay his debts.

I try to imagine this great frenzy of painting. For five years he produced an average of fifty paintings a year. That is almost a picture a week. He shipped them off to London: dock scenes, street scenes, moonlights. Many, many dock scenes for the board rooms of industrialists; many, many moonlights. City streets for the salons of city bankers. Mansions for the dwellers in gothic mansions.

After five years, we are told, he began to be oppressed by a sense of failure. His children rode in a carriage with silver harness from which, however, they could not dismount because they had no boots. His paintings show marks of haste and careless handling. He sometimes painted over photographs.

In the summer of 1890 he invited journalists into his basement studio to witness how, by projecting a photograph from a magic lantern, he could cast an image on canvas over which he ran his pencil to produce the outline of a suburban lane. This, he explained, saved valuable time and speeded up production.

That is how I picture him, standing at his canvas: that is where I see him most clearly of all. He is small and frail; at fifty-four he still wears a fair moustache. He has the appearance of a chronic consumptive. He is increasingly oppressed by a sense of failure. He is sick of the treadmill, of the public hunger for moonlights. The lane projected by the magic lantern is one of the many lanes in a labyrinth in which he has lost his way.

彩

A woman's figure stands at a bend in the road. Tree shadows on the wall succeed hers like sentinels: landmarks she has left behind, or sinister followers. There is no moon; but the tree branches, touched by moonlight, are picked out to the smallest twig.

A woman's figure stands at a bend in the road. Drifts of leaves follow her. It is sunset; lamps are burning in the windows of the tall house. There is a door in the wall, but it is barred with brambles: it has not been opened now for many years.

A woman's figure stands at a bend in the road. She carries a basket. A green moon hangs among cirrus clouds. Lamps are lit in the windows of the tall house, but they are not for her. She is moving past, beyond, out of the picture. Her back is towards us, her face invisible.

Where has she come from, where is she going to? It is a mystery without meaning, a parable without clues. Our eyes eat the picture, searching for symbols. We see what we most wish to: mother, lover, muse.

彩

I do not know why it is that I still want to please her. Why, all these years after her death, I still pursue her down endless hospital corridors, down twisting lanes of dreams in which I never quite catch up with her retreating back.

Once, when I was a boy, we walked home at midnight through deserted streets, through a pall of gunpowder and the smoke of bonfires, our faces tingling with November frost: back to the safety of home, to the warm glow behind windows. We held hands and swung them slightly. Her face, touched by silver, was entirely beautiful.

And again, that time she stood in the back garden by starlight, in her white night-gown, taking in washing she said, although there was no washing: as she went through the motions in a strange miming dance, then too she appeared to me quite beautiful.

Her face, swollen with steroids, hangs like a great moon in my imagination. I can't see past it. I have never succeeded in painting it.

※

No paintings have been discovered from the year 1891. By 1891, we must assume, he was exhausted. But in 1892 he began again. Seascapes, snowscapes, beach scenes: his palette torn by gashes of dazzling light.

After years of moonlight he must have been blinded by so much sun. His eyes were failing: the doctor forbade him his brushes, forced him to rest. But soon he was up again, seduced by all that white snow. He rushed into it like a child, there was no stopping him. Ill and in debt, he remained at his work until he could stand no longer. At NIght he crawled on his hands and knees to bed, to the Persian brass bed with the silk hangings.

His daughter read Browning and Tennyson at his bedside. His wife sat silently and held his hand.

I cannot escape the image of his last days wrapped in light, in the false light with which death deceives us; and of his last pictures, empty white expanses tokening oblivion; and of the brilliant peacock feathers with their painted eyes; and of his final acknowledgment of the coming darkness: "No sun, no moon, no stars."

※

Five years after his death there was a generous retrospective. In 1912 a job lot including 'Moonlight' fetched one and a half guineas at an auction sale.

Four decades later the widow of an industrialist sent a batch of his paintings to a sale at Leeds, received no bid, chopped them up and burned them.

In 1960 the city council applied for special permission to clear the cemetery in which he lay buried along with his eight infant children. The headstones were removed, the ground smoothed and grassed, and a garden of remembrance planted on the site of his forgotten tomb.

That same year the assistant keeper hung a picture called 'Golden Light' in the entrance hall of a provincial gallery. He hung it there because he liked the look of it. He could not have foretold how dock scenes and street scenes would be unearthed from attics, how long-forgotten heirlooms would be revealed; how lanes and lakes, beaches and bridges, ships and mansions would rise from heaps of lumber in a fabulous resurrection of lost paintings.

※

I have to acknowledge now that I will always be associated with him. The catalogue, the hardback, the biography, are all mine. My name, through its attachment to that of another, has acquired the vague familiarity of a man of minor fame.

People write to me sometimes. Heartfelt letters. They tell me what it is about him that appeals to them.

Sometimes they ask me what it is about him that appeals to me.

I do not answer them entirely truthfully.

I tell them I admire his handling and his eye for detail. His use of colour and his use of light. The air of mystery which hangs over his paintings, which although figurative and limited, nevertheless retain a ghostlike charm.

All this is true. But I do not tell them the real reason why I seek out his work. Why I will travel miles, to obscure galleries and private salons, merely to obtain a glimpse of something I have, to all intents and purposes, seen before. I re-enter the labyrinth; once more I am standing in the moonlight of his endless dream. I am as lost as he is. And it fills me with wonder, that failure can be so beautiful.

A New Story for Nada

This is not an old story. This is a new story, about the way I am now. There is no point in reading those old stories any more. I could give them to you, but you wouldn't learn anything about me from them.

Sometimes I think I give people the old stories in order to protect myself, to prevent them from finding out who I really am. Those stories are safe and complete, they are polished and published. They hold not one scrap of danger, not one glimmer of discovery. They are so old now I have left them far behind, they live in another life, they breathe in another country. Their ashes are dead, their passions are burned out, I feel nothing for them any more, I no longer have any feeling.

All afternoon you stood in the light of the window and told me "I feel this," "I think that," "I know what you are saying. Yes, I understand." Sometimes you stood and sometimes you sat down. We drank tea from thick white cups with no ornamentation. But always you remained in the light of the window, turned away slightly from it, the dull light of the window a halo behind your head.

I have spent my whole life looking out of windows. I cannot see a window without looking at the view. Whenever I think of a woman I think of a woman gazing out of a window. She doesn't know where to take herself, she doesn't know what to do.

You didn't look out of your window, you are bored with that view. You glanced at it occasionally with tired eyes. You drew your feet up onto the chair, your knees to your chest. When you had finished your tea you lit a cigarette. I didn't talk to you about views and windows. I told you I had spent my whole life waiting for the post.

A long, long time ago our parents made mistakes. You and I were both accidents. Now we see that our parents were also people. "She was young, she was only a girl. How could she know any better?"

You are talking about your own history, about your own mother. My history is different, I and my dead mother have different issues. My problem is not forgiveness, it is understanding.

"But there are some things," I say. "In an intelligent person..." You look at me with large eyes, you are rather shocked. "There are some things I will never understand about my mother." You have no idea what I am referring to.

Your son is shouting in the next room. I don't know what I feel about him. He is laughing with his friend in the kitchen. I have always been nervous and afraid of children.

"But what I want to know," you say. "I'll tell you what is really bugging me." He opens the study door without knocking. "Mum, where did you put my protectors?"

"They're on the side in the kitchen."

He shakes his head.

"Well then they're under the kitchen table."

He shakes his head.

"Are you sure?" You go and look for them.

You come back laughing, "I told Jason he was an accident."

I don't have accidents, I don't make mistakes. I am too cautious. My life is circumscribed by the safe and familiar. I don't visit China, I don't book cheap flights, I don't go for acupuncture or aromatherapy. I don't abseil or do parachute drops or talk to strangers. If I change the route of my walk it is a grand adventure.

Lately I have taken to buying different clothes. Striped T-shirts, denim jackets, boot-cut jeans. I put in my contact lenses, polish my shoes, dress carefully when I am coming to visit you.

You tell me to live wildly, take risks, not be afraid of people. I tell you I carry my life like water in the palm of my hand, that even the new route of my walk stuns me with its beauty.

"Yes," you say, "yes, I can see that," pulling on your cigarette. You are not convinced.

Your house is on a steep slope covered in trees. Your garden is a series of terraces. You step from terrace to terrace in mules and a thin brown sweater. The line of your cigarette follows you, a thin trail of smoke.

Everywhere you have made little stations, little arbours for yourself. A bench and a pot plant, a fountain with a wisteria. Nothing more than toeholds on the sheer hillside.

Your garden is dank and cool, the large leaves flutter; there have been almost no sunny days for you to sit out this summer. Ever since you have lived in this house you have been unhappy.

There are fresh pink blooms on the azalea: each time you go out you notice something new. You touch the blooms of the azalea, push back your hair, stand with one elbow cupped in the palm of your hand. Still smoking. You do not belong here. You belong in a hot country.

A long long time ago you came here from somewhere else. Now, like the rest of us, you can never go back, nor can you ever belong in this cold country.

Your English is sleepy and accented; sometimes you struggle for words, you make mistakes. I have never heard you speak in your own language.

You tell me about a boy in your grandmother's village who is a man now, older than you, who still asks after you and who never married.

I also do not belong, though you wouldn't know it. I have a love-hate relationship with my perfect English. Far longer ago than you, my father came to this country, and when I was born he filled me with his own homesickness.

Somewhere long ago and far away is a boy you are frightened of seeing again, whom you might have married. Somewhere far in my past is a girl who wanted to marry her father.

Later you bring the tail end of a bottle of wine. Two glasses. "I don't like to drink alone," you say.

I take the smaller glass. You don't argue.

Your study, your office, I say, is a pleasant space. It has bookshelves, a blondwood floor, two desks and three windows. A black stove which doesn't throw out much heat. The desks are swamped in papers, the shelves are crammed; there are heaps of files and samples on the floor. You say you can't work in here, the space is wrong: you can't see the shape of the page, the face of the paper.

Years ago I discovered the place I needed to write: up under the roof, in a small corner, a high garret with a sloping ceiling so low you almost banged your head against it.

You like to write on trains, in cafés, on park benches. You think of renting a flat, of buying a boat. For years you have been looking for the right room to write in: a room the house doesn't possess, which doesn't exist.

There's no doubt about it, you are very tactile. Everyone notices, they all remark on it. Within moments of meeting a person you will have your hand on their knee. You hugged me good-bye like a sister the first time we met.

Your eyes, which you say are mould-green, hold mine often during our conversation.

"So, what do you want, what is bugging you, what is on your mind?"

I stand close to the stove. I am cold. I don't answer.

For my birthday three weeks ago you gave me a special gift: a volume of Chekhov and a new outfit. The Chekhov bore an inscription in your dashed handwriting. The outfit was summery: a pair of white calf-length trousers and a blue checked blouse.

The giftwrap was pink and girlish and covered in lingerie cartoons. Corset, suspender, mini, corset, G-string, bra. They made me laugh. I said, "My husband will laugh his head off when he sees this."

When I showed my husband the giftwrap he didn't laugh. He frowned and said it was ridiculous.

I didn't show him the outfit. I hung it up in the cupboard. I haven't tried on my new outfit yet.

On the wall of your office is a photograph of yourself aged eighteen. The year you came to London you took it in a photo-booth. Your mother enlarged and framed it and kept it in her flat in Zagreb. When your mother died last year you took it and hung it on your office wall.

Your hair and eyes are dark, you are wearing a dark beret. Your cheeks are full. I don't recognise your eyes.

I search the picture and I glance at your face. You watch me looking at the photograph. Your face is grave, but your eyes do not betray you. I see a pretty girl, not necessarily innocent. She reminds me of the girl I loved once, when I was eleven.

People don't know why you married the man you did. They are always asking you: Why did you marry him? You laugh, you blow smoke, you shrug your shoulders. "Why does one marry? It's all a compromise. There's no such thing as the perfect relationship."

I say, "I think sometimes my husband is jealous of my women friends."

"Yes," you say. "Mine too. I can understand that." Another thing you are able to understand.

You fetch me a book from the shelves, a book with a photograph of two Edwardian ladies embracing stiffly on the cover, a book which falls open at a painting of two naked voluptuous women sleeping on a couch: photos of Gertrude Stein and Alice B. Toklas, snaps of Thelma Wood and Djuna Barnes. I leaf through the pages half-smiling, half-bemused; I wonder what you are up to. My wineglass is empty; the wine has gone to my head. I flip through the pages but the spine is broken. It always falls open at the same place. I feel sudden prickles of self-consciousness. You watch me looking at the photographs.

You like to put the cat amongst the pigeons. You tell me this has always been your way. You like to challenge people, find out what they are made of. You ask direct questions, play devil's advocate.

The first time you told me this I was annoyed. I don't like being provoked or manipulated. The stuff I'm made of is my own business.

I turn my empty wineglass and weigh my words carefully. I can feel my heart beating. I'm thinking of saying things I may regret later. "Why will you regret them?" Because I always do.

The condition of the writer is like this: the writer never knows what they are really feeling. The writer is a full-time actress, always performing the part of what her characters might feel.

For many years now my life has been a performance. Ever since I remember I have chosen my own role.

I confide in nobody. Nobody can be trusted.

Nevertheless, my heart is beating and I think of saying things I will certainly regret. I am sorry about the wine, I wish I had not drunk it. You do not press me, however. I put the book aside.

For a long time now I have been cold, very cold and rigid, capable of nothing. Do not enter my landscape: all you will find there is a bleak Antarctica.

You tell me to take risks, live wildly, open myself to people. I tell you if I were not so timid I would live differently.

You are content with my assessment, you think I am cold and timid. You believe I am frozen and rigid and full of snow.

The truth is (and this is the truth) I am Vesuvius. Beneath the ice there is lava. Watch your step.

How do I live? Like a statue, maintaining the same poise, staying the same way year after frozen year, expressing myself in small pieces which never begin to simulate the whole.

How do I live? On a slow burn, eating myself up inside, my head swarming with images from the big picture. It's a killer jigsaw. I live entirely in my imagination.

Sometimes I think I could erupt, get physical, say things I would regret later. But it would never happen. The actuality of you would always come between me and any real feeling.

You stretch your limbs like a cat: you are the sort of person my mother would have disapproved of. The sort of person who drinks wine in the afternoons.

You shake back your hair, your eyes are a cat's green. You have a catlike nature, I think: a feline affection.

You like to keep cats. You are a cat person.

You ask so much and no more; you push so far and no further. You start but you don't finish. Why do you do it? You're curious like a cat, but you are also cautious. I think the ice is in me, but perhaps it's in you.

You are never too old to play games, but you are old enough, now, to get weary. Ever since your mother's death you have been more conscious than ever of your own mortality.

You said to me once, in the car, after a hot flush, "I'm falling apart, darling. Soon nobody will even want to look at me." You described all your symptoms to an older friend. "'Darling,' she said, 'that's *nothing*! That's only the beginning.'"

I am reaching the age now where I make friends with older women. They teach me the most important thing: that it is possible to go forward. My friends are my guidelights into the unknown darkness. Fifty next year, you are more beautiful than ever.

I wonder what my friendship means to you. You said you wanted a mentor. You wanted someone to share the terrible burden of your creativity.

I am afraid of living up to your expectations. I give off an air of wisdom, a genetic characteristic inherited from my father.

We are exact opposites. The impulsive and the pedantic; the sensualist and the nun. I gaze in wonder on your sea of chaos; you gaze in wonder on my field of discipline.

You no longer expect me to take your cigarettes.

When we talk of art we are breathing the same smoke.

Now we are both clock-watchers: you because of your son and I because of my husband. The hours fly by when we are together.

I always wonder when we will meet again.

You are the sort of person who wants to give something when she parts—a rose, a recipe, a poetry book. I don't often leave here empty-handed. You say, "You must read this. Read it." You press something of yours upon me, but it isn't truly yours, it bears no real imprint, it is impersonal.

I would like to take home the hat we bought together, which makes you look like a ringmistress and makes me look like a seminarian.

I would like to take the hat which we took turns wearing, in the bric-à-brac shop, in front of the old mirror. You would miss it while it was gone; and when you came to see me I could give it back again.

This is not an old story. This is a new story, about the way I am now. I have written it for you because I am sick of the old stories. I am ready for fresh pastures, hungry for something new.

But now that I look at the story I see it is not as new as I thought: it is full of old tropes and familiar symbols, full of the same conflicts and the same questions, framed in the same language I both love and hate.

There in the middle of the story I am still sitting. What am I made of? Have you found out yet?

A Letter from Josef K.

I

t is many years now since I went to prison. You must have forgotten all about me. Perhaps you thought I was dead. I would not have blamed you: at one time I thought I was dead myself. I fully anticipated a death sentence. Instead, to my bewilderment, I found myself condemned to life.

What is it like? The first few months passed in a haze. For weeks I was hardly able to eat, and since I was already thin when I came, I must have been reduced almost to a shadow. I remember being amazed at the stick-legs and twig-arms I thrust into my clothes of a morning. All the more astonishing is my transformation, when I look down at myself now and see I have grown so fat.

Yes, I am well and truly settled. I have adjusted to the routine, in fact I couldn't survive without it. Apart from giving each day its sense of purpose, it makes the time pass a lot more quickly. Since this is a life-term, one hardly knows why one should wish it to; nevertheless one does. In spite of all the comforts, the knowledge remains that you are still a prisoner, and you never quite lose that residual longing to be free.

To an outsider, prison life would not seem to be a hardship.

Apart from having to follow the general pattern of meals, exercise and sleep to which everyone must conform, I am not made to do anything at all. As soon as I was able, I was offered a choice of improving or useful occupations, courses of study, even a bit of paid work. I tried a little bag-making and a little cookery. But once I discovered the library I wanted nothing else. The library here is simply enormous: light and airy, and filled with more books than one could read in a single lifetime. Since one lifetime is all I have, I read incessantly.

There is no need to make contact with my fellow readers. We sit alone at the big tables, or in private alcoves, in an almost holy silence broken only by the turning of pages and the occasional scrape of a chair. The same faces appear daily at the same places, for prison has turned us all into creatures of habit. Number 21172, a man with prominent teeth, sits diagonally opposite me and prefers Westerns, while directly before me number 41055, a girl with kiss-curls at her temples, dreams over her books and hardly turns the pages. By shifting slightly in my chair I may catch sight of the bearded pedagogue who haunts the Natural History section; while I myself will probably never budge from Jurisprudence. Having grown familiar, my companions generally vanish, released in turn from the prison where I must remain for ever. One alone seems likely to outlast me: a young man with the face of a New Testament saint in one of the more sentimental Italian paintings, who reads as assiduously as I, and who I am convinced, from his air of sad serenity, must be a lifer like myself.

But more often than not I read in the privacy of my own cell. This is frowned on by the authorities, of course. I know I am regarded as an unsociable creature. I take my meals alone and maintain a monkish solitude. Yet for the first year or so nothing would have induced me to stay in my cell more than was necessary, nor even to shut the door. The reason for this was perfectly simple, and common to nearly all the prisoners: we are naturally terrified of being locked in. The doors do, after all, possess locks, of which the warders carry the keys. And while one seldom or never hears of any prisoner being literally imprisoned in their cell, nonetheless, the possibility remains. There is hardly anyone among us, consequently, who does not suffer from claustrophobia. During my first months here I would wake several times a night, in a sweat of panic, and try the door. It never was locked, but a long time passed before I developed sufficient confidence to enter my cell willingly and close it behind me.

That hurdle being surmounted, however, I now enjoy all the privacy I want, except for the inevitable attentions of my warder. It is a nuisance, but even I can't deny the necessity of warders in what is, after all, a prison. They are numerous, both male and female; they sleep on the premises, share our meals and join in the standard activities, so that to all intents and purposes they are prisoners like ourselves, except that they carry the keys. My own is a man of about my age, sandy-haired, pleasant-faced, invariably kind and courteous; I am aware, however, that his goodwill depends on my co-operation. Such privileges as my own cell, private washing facilities, and the rich food which has made me sleek, are obtained through his efforts, and often at some cost to himself. We have known each other so long now, and so intimately, that we talk almost like an old married couple. But there is no doubt as to who holds the balance of power. When he came to me on my first night—and let me tell you, when I arrived here I was an utter virgin—I was beyond bewilderment, resistance was futile, I was invaded and laid waste body and soul. The second time I resisted more powerfully, not being taken by surprise; on which occasion he relented. Since then he has never forced his attentions, and yet I have found it impossible to refuse him. With his tales of woe about the hardships of a warder's life, he has convinced me that to be a guard is a far worse fate than to be a prisoner. I feel an obligation to provide him with what comfort I can, and since this brief and muffled act, so furtive, absurd and hopeless, seems to satisfy him, I don't withhold myself. I have passed through all the gradations of fear, anger and disgust, to this final indifference, so that his nighttime visits have become more tedious than upsetting, and by morning they are usually forgotten.

Of course, I am not the only one to submit to these indignities. In fact I would say the majority of us do, though they are never spoken of. I could approach the governor at any time and ask for my warder to be changed; he wouldn't refuse me. But since his replacement would be just as likely to expect favours, and might be less agreeable, I don't suppose I shall ever take that step.

Apart from my warder, then, I have little to do with other human beings, and am quite content to stay in my cell, which has become a home to me. We are all permitted to decorate our cells as we please, within a certain budget, and I have done mine in white and yellow, which I consider to be a positive colour. I have plants, and some well-chosen items of furniture; not many ornaments, for I despise clutter, and of course, a well-stocked book-case. None of these things belong to me, but it is difficult to imagine them belonging to anyone else. I can be sure that, for the period of my tenancy, they won't be taken from me, so they are as good as mine.

The maintenance of my little home has become one of my chief delights, and I am rather proud to think that it has drawn the admiration of the governor himself, when he has passed through on inspection. Some prisoners lose all interest in their surroundings when they enter prison, and though we are all required to keep our cells clean and tidy, there are those who make no effort to disguise the fact that they are living in an institution by covering the walls, hanging curtains at the windows or keeping a few personal items on display. I pity them: since we must be here, we may as well make ourselves comfortable, and my interest in interior decoration has served to distract me from many a more gloomy thought.

In recent years I have taken up another interest, namely gardening. It is remarkable what a sympathy one can develop with growing, rooted things. Although we take a period of exercise in the prison yard each day, it was a long time before I could work up the courage to take a strip of garden for myself. My fear of the open air may seem absurd and paradoxical, as indeed is so much of prison life. The truth is, after my initial terror of being enclosed, I developed an almost childish dependence on that enclosure and safety. The outside world began to seem a place of danger, of lurking unfamiliar terrors. The soil itself, the first time I handled it, was something primitive and alien: I dreaded discovering a worm or encountering a beetle, so long had I been in the exclusive company of humans, and increasingly, of just myself.

But I got over this, and now I have a fine garden growing. A good deal of my time is taken up with seed catalogues, manuals, and articles in the Sunday supplements; and whenever I begin to feel the walls pressing in on me, as they still do sometimes, I will run out into the allotments, rain or shine, and do a half-hour's work. My plants, after all, are the only children I will ever have, and if they regard me, prisoner number 11414, as a sort of parent, my efforts will have been amply rewarded.

While digging in the allotments I have often noticed—it was no secret to me—how the gates of the prison stand open, and the constant to and fro of traffic on the main access road. These are the vehicles which bring us food, new books and fresh laundry, and which take away our refuse, the products of our prison workshops, and sometimes the prisoners themselves, when their appearance is required in Court. Everything is most efficiently run, to the degree that beyond those open gates there seems to lie a completely chaotic world. And yet that world is freedom, after all, the gates do lie open and there is only the most desultory guard. Nor is one obliged to use the gates: our prison, far from being enclosed by high fences, barbed wire and watchtowers, is surrounded only by a low hedge and an abundance of honeysuckle.

Given these circumstances, a free person might well ask why I don't take the opportunity to escape. It is the sort of question only a free person would be capable of asking. They would never find themselves in here in the first place, or if they did, they'd be across those fields within the hour: and most likely none of the guards would stop them. For me it is different. An outsider, lacking understanding, might say, "Of your own free will you entered this place, and of your own free will you may leave it." But the truth is I have lost my will, and did so on the day I was imprisoned here.

During my first years here I received occasional visits from my sister, who was always agitated, and demanded to know why I did not make any effort to escape. It was quite impossible to explain to her that my case had been tried and sentence passed, that it was our duty to accept the judgement of the Court, otherwise what would become of justice? True enough, it remains a source of wonder to me how prisoners, day after day, can walk through the gates of the prison as free as air, their terms having been served (there have even been rumours of parole for some) but this will never be my fate, and my sister, when she finally understood as much, ceased to come.

Meanwhile, I am not unhappy, or, if I am, it is only that unhappiness I mentioned earlier: the longing for a lost freedom. I often ask myself whether it is possible for one so utterly condemned to feel a moment's joy; and yet, it is undeniable, there have been moments in my garden, or when gazing at the walls of my pretty cell, when I have experienced a profound contentment. Nevertheless, to be relieved of the responsibilities of daily life, out there in the world, is no consolation when one is so completely subject, so without independence or prospects of any kind.

When the recollection of this becomes more than I can bear, I take refuge in the library, where I can at least travel in imagination to those lands I will never visit. I like to think my fellow readers do the same. This morning I noticed that my old companion, the saint, was no longer sitting in his accustomed seat. I made enquiries: the idea of his having been released filled me with a cold dread, for then I should really have been the only lifer. Ah, but there is more than one way to leave the prison. He had died in the night; it is the ultimate fate of lifers, and a considerable number of us leave so.

Acknowledgements

The stories in this collection first appeared as follows, some in a slightly different form:

'Return to Zion' in *Stand* vol. 39 no. 4
'Kafka in Brontëland' in *The Slow Mirror: New Fiction by Jewish Writers* edited by Sonja Lyndon and Sylvia Paskin (Five Leaves Press) and in *Leviathan Three* edited by Jeff VanderMeer and Forrest Aguirre (Ministry of Whimsy Press)
'The Other Mr Perella' in *Panurge* no. 23
'The Girlfriend' in *Writing Women* 10/3
'Dr Stein' in *Metropolitan* no. 8
'Uncle Oswald' in *The Jewish Quarterly* no. 169
'Mrs Rubin and her Daughter' in *Staple* no. 40
'An Italian Child' in *Staple* no. 37
'Waiting for Rain' in *Writing Women* 12/3
'Mr Applewick' in *London Magazine* 33/9 & 10 and in *Best Short Stories*, edited by Giles Gordon and David Hughes (Heinemann)
'Moonlight' in *Leviathan Quarterly* no. 2 and in *Leviathan Three* (Ministry of Whimsy Press)
'A New Story for Nada' in *Leviathan Quarterly* no. 7

About the Author

Tamar Yellin

Tamar Yellin was born in the north of England. Her mother was the daughter of a Polish immigrant and her father a third generation Jerusalemite. She studied Hebrew and Arabic at Oxford, where she received the Pusey and Ellerton Prize for Biblical Hebrew. She has since worked as a teacher and lecturer in Judaism, and as a Jewish Faith Visitor in schools across Yorkshire. She began writing fiction at an early age, and the creative tension between her Jewish heritage and her Yorkshire Roots has informed much of her work. Her short stories, which have been described as "ironic, humane and highly accomplished," have appeared in a wide variety of journals and anthologies. This is the first time they appear in book form. She has published one novel, *The Genizah at the House of Shepher,* also with Toby Press.

The fonts used in this book are from the Garamond family

Other works by Tamar Yellin
available from *The* Toby Press

The Genizah at the House of Shepher

The Toby Press publishes fine writing,
available at leading bookstores everywhere. For more
information, please visit www.tobypress.com